BLOOD PASSION
BOOK VI
Family of Vampire

J.M. VALENTE
Cover design by J.M. Valente

Gotham Books

30 N Gould St.
Ste. 20820, Sheridan, WY 82801
https://gothambooksinc.com/

Phone: 1 (307) 464-7800

© 2025 *J.M. Valente*. All rights reserved.

No part of this book may be reproduced, stored in a retrieval system, or transmitted by any means without the written permission of the author.

Published by Gotham Books (April 3, 2025)

ISBN: 979-8-3492-4056-0 (H)
ISBN: 979-8-3492-4054-6 (P)
ISBN: 979-8-3492-4055-3 (E)

Because of the dynamic nature of the Internet, any web addresses or links contained in this book may have changed since publication and may no longer be valid.

The views expressed in this work are solely those of the author and do not necessarily reflect the views of the publisher, and the publisher hereby disclaims any responsibility for them.

TABLE OF CONTENTS

REVIEW/PRAISE iv
BLOOD PASSION BOOK VI v
Acknowledgments vi
Dedication vii

CHAPTERS
1. 1
2. 5
3. 9
4. 13
5. 18
6. 22
7. 25
8. 29
9. 34
10. 40
11. 43
12. 46
13. 49
14. 53
15. 57
16. 61
17. 66
18. 70
19. 74
20. 78
21. 83
22. 87
23. 91
24. 94
25. 98
26. 104
27. 107
28. 111
29. 114
30. 119
Epilogue 125

REVIEW/PRAISE

'Blood Passion-Book VI-Family of Vampire is the continuation of a mesmerizing plunge into a world where the boundary between humans and Vampires blurs in the shadows of Sleepy Hollow, New York. This gothic thriller by author J.M. Valente is a chilling and enthralling journey that delves deep into the darkest corners of human nature and the macabre allure of Vampirism. Valente crafts a mesmerizing world where the boundaries between humans and Vampires are not just blurred but magnificently intertwined. The story centers on Rachael Valli, a compelling character who is a half-human, half-vampire Hybrid. Born from a forbidden union, Rachael navigates a life straddling two worlds—each with its own set of rules, prejudices, and expectations. Valente does an exceptional job of delving into Rachael's internal struggles, portraying her as a character who is neither fully one nor the other but a poignant embodiment of both. Her Vampire lover Victor adds a rich layer to the narrative. Rachael and Victor are not just predators; they are individuals confronting their private demons, and this introspective approach adds a layer of philosophical depth to the thriller. Valente skillfully illustrates the complexities of their bond, highlighting both the passion and the sacrifices involved.'

J.M. Valente's
BLOOD PASSION BOOK VI
Family of Vampire

is an absolute triumph in modern gothic-type Tragic Love Story-telling, combining atmospheric tension with a thought-provoking narrative. It is a gripping read for fans of this type of genre, offering a fresh take on Vampire lore while maintaining the dark elegance and suspense that defines a truly great modern gothic thriller. Valente's novel is a haunting reminder of the power of darkness and the complexities that lie within the human soul.

Jeannie Scott Flynn

Acknowledgments

My thanks once again go to
to my Beta reader, Jeannie Scott Flynn, for keeping me inspired in my writings.

And a special thanks
to Producer Jim Burgoa and Actress Andrea Garcia for the silhouette picture of them taken by Jim's Dad, Fabian.
Which inspired the cover and title page graphics.
Plus to my Grammarly Editing Program,
also my amazon Fire tablet.

Dedication

*To all my faithful Fans,
of all my Published Novels!*

1.

Victor Is Comfortably seated in one of the chairs in the shaded area near the side door in the Lobby of the Riverside Bed and Breakfast Inn, in the town of Sleepy Hollow, New York State, just having a quick glance through a magazine that someone had left on the small table beside him. While Mike is working at the Inns' Registration counter. He takes a short break from this work, and he lifts his head, removes his reading glasses and rubs the bridge of his nose, looks over to Victor where he is seated, and inquires of him,

"Hey, Victor, you thinking of getting yourself a Motorcycle?"

"How did you…" He stops and turns the magazine over, looking at the large picture of the Motorcycle on the cover, and continues, "Wow, Mike, you must have good vision! You can see what's on the cover from way over there."

"Well, Victor, I only need these glasses for reading; otherwise my vision is excellent, and it is a rather large picture of a very nice Harley Davidson Motorcycle on the cover, and I do remember that Ben had left it there on the table right beside you, so I just figured it to be the one you must be looking through since it is the only one that was there on that table. We're not in the practice of keeping an assortment of magazines in the Lobby."

"Yes, Mike, you figured right, and I was thinking of getting one, not too sure Rachael would approve of me buying it, though."

"Okay, then don't ask her if you can; just suggest you possibly buy one and see what she says and then take it from there."

"Well, Mike, I did say something like that not too long ago, but she didn't respond. Still, that seems to me like some good sound advice."

"Great, then give it a shot and see how she reacts, and Victor, I've been meaning to ask you something, if it's not too bold. Where are you from? You seem to have a northern accent, so I just was wondering."

"I am from Atlanta, Georgia, but was educated up in the Chicago, Illinois school system and their University of Archaeology, so I don't actually have much of a Southern accent; I guess I have the Windy City one."

"Really wouldn't know; I don't think I've ever heard one."

"Well, you have now!"

At that moment, Ben shows up in the Lobby from the kitchen to franticly ask,

"Mike, Mike, you seen my Cycle Mag anywhere out here?"

"Calm down, my boy, yes I have," He points at Victor and answers Ben, saying,

"Victor's looking through it."

He then takes his station on the Lobby bench and says,

"I think I'll wait till he finishes with it."

Victor hears Ben and Mike talking, so he gets up and walks to where they are, holding out the magazine to Ben, informing him,

"Here you go, my boy, just giving it a quick look through is all."

"You like Harleys, Mr. Vincent Sir?"

"Ben, what'd I tell you about calling me, Sir? And Mr. Vincent is my father. But, as I have told you, I am Victor, so you will address me as such, please."

"Oh yup, I forgot; it will be Victor from now on for sure."

"See to it, please, see you two later on, for lunch."

Victor replies to Ben's inquiry as he's making his way up the stairs to the second floor,

"And to answer your question about my interest in Harley Davidson Motorcycles, Ben, yes, I do like them very much; I knew someone that drove a very nice one, just thinking of getting one for myself."

Ben turns to Mike, who is getting back to his work, and states,

"Wow, Mike, just think? Victor on a Harley now would be really cool! Almost as cool as Angel, and speaking of Angel, I was wondering how she is doing in the place you sent her to."

"Ben, speaking of her, I'm pretty sure you've been thinking of her, I have not heard from her or the Inn she is at, so things must be okay."

"You are probably right, Mike! I just wish she was staying here with us."

"Me too, but we are all full up!"

Ben sadly replies to him as he walks out the side door with his magazine, to sit on the Deck to look at it and dream of having one for himself someday.

"Yup, I know Mike, I know."

Jeannie comes into the Lobby, irately asking of Mike,

"Brother, have you seen Benjamin around anywhere? He left the kitchen abruptly, and I still have some prep work for the lunch meal for him to do!"

"Sis, he is out on the Deck reading his Motorcycle magazine."

"Please, tell him I need him in the kitchen pronto."

"Yes, sis, as soon as I can, lots of paperwork to catch up on still."

"But, Mike, I really need him ASAP!"

Mike sharply puts down his pen, comes out from behind the counter, and replies, as he makes a start for the side door.

"Yup, I hear you, sis; I'll go out and tell him right now."

She thanks him and returns quickly to the kitchen.

Mike slightly opens the door and tells Ben that his sister, Chef Jeannie needs him back in the kitchen. He responds in somewhat reluctant diligence; sluggishly, he enters the Inns' Lobby to go to the kitchen. Finally, Mike releases the door to let it close, and he goes back to his work.

In the moments that coincide with the most recent interactions at the Riverside Bed and Breakfast Inn, and elsewhere on Planet Earth, up in Angel's room at the Ichabod Crane B&B Inn, also in the town of Sleepy Hollow, New York State, a bright white light appears seemingly from nowhere; from this light steps out an unearthly prominent, formidable ethereal figure that has the appearance of an Earthly Human male. It gradually becomes tangible, miraculously now having all the knowledge of what has transpired and what it is to do; as of this very moment, and the moments prior to this, his place in this world has been preordained in his understanding, and to others, as someone, they all knew as Angel Seraph a U.S. Marshal Special Agent, but now know and have been known as Michael T. A. Aggelos the U.S. Marshal Special Agent. For she has been erased, as was afore communicated to her, Angel's substitution: this tall, dark, handsome Earth-like male who will be known and recognized to most as simply Michael but almost only to him as her substitution. Also, seemingly overnight, and undetected by anyone, a black Harley Davidson

Motorcycle appeared in the parking lot of the Inn, which is looked upon as something that has been there for a few days now, which means that it is not unusual to be there in the parking space assigned for what is, as of now and before, Michael's room.

As far as expectantly anyone knew or will know, from this moment on, Michael is and has been the occupant of this room at the Inn for a few days now. Solely he trusts he is the only one that knows the truth in all that has transpired, now meaning that he has all the knowledge of all the time spent and the things that Angel accomplished in her approved requested life on and in this Earthly plane of existence. Even the position of being the U.S. Marshal Special Agent is now known to be held by Michael, not Angel, from the beginning of her installment into the Agency of the U.S. Marshals. It is now and forever believed by most that Angel never even existed; intending that all memories of her have been obliterated from most people's minds and replaced by knowing this Michael individual who has now taken over her labors of the very noble cause for being here on this Earthly world that genuinely needs someone like this for their protection against actually and potentially Malevolent unearthly forces.

Except for two extraordinarily unique persons; Rachael Valli and Victor Vincent, who are not entirely Human, they are completely unaware that something unearthly and powerful has blocked this from happening to their minds. They and only them will now exclusively retain their remembrances and associations with; an individual very well, currently and formerly, known to them as Angel Seraph, operating as a U.S. Marshal, Special Agent.

The powers that be and have control; are unaware that not all the minds and memories of everyone concurrently involved have been altered in the way of their latest Grand Design; in their efforts to continue protecting the Humans of this Planet Earth.

2.

U.S. Marshal Michael, sits in his dimly lit room at the Ichabod Crain Inn, after looking in the closet to find some, if not all, of Angel's Earthly trappings and most of her weapons in her Rucksack. The one item he removes, he has a tremendous interest in is this unique old Novel, *'The Nine Doors to the Domain of Darkness'* then he puts the Rucksack back in the closet. Now he sits, turns on the bright light on the table next to him, and casually opens it to the first engraving, thinking,

All the copies of this Malicious, scarce, and ancient Novel were believed to have been destroyed long ago.

All though he does have all of Angel's memories of attaining it from the Satanic Cult in upper state New York, he also realizes, as she did, that this item must be disposed of in a way that it can no longer be used for the Malevolent purpose it was created and intended for.

As he slowly closes the book, in his lap and then lays his hand upon it, a revivifying light gradually appears in a darkened corner of his room. It was believed that all the copies of this Novel being rather Evil and very ancient, were destroyed long ago along with its collaborating mortal author.

Suddenly an indistinguishable shadowy entity inside a bright light, although not an earthly image, speaks to him within his mind,

'Michael, take this Evil and grievous item down to the River's edge and burn it utterly, then cast its ashes into the rolling waters, so that it may never be obtained by anyone in this Earthly world ever again.'

Michael answers aloud,

"That was precisely what I had in mind to do with it, as is said on this Earthly plane. 'Great minds do think alike.'

'Yes, now perform this deed post haste, and then take up the tasks that Angel Seraph had initiated.'

Michael answers aloud again,

"Yes, what it is now very clear to me; I do feel a call for a fresh mission is coming to me, soon."

And with that said, the light slowly fades away, and that corner of Michaels' room goes dark again.

Michael opens the closet door to once again bring out Angel Seraphs' Rucksack, to have a more analytic look at what she has left behind, now laying out the items on the bed; one semi-automatic Shotgun and a 45 Magnum handgun with a holster, loaded with silver ammo and three boxes of the same, a small leather bag filled with some Shotgun shells, a silver knife in a holster sheath, and an empty pint bottle of Wild Turkey 150 proof Bourbon whiskey, also another book; one that seems un impressive titled 'Mystic Vampyres' by Mia Harkness, and the other book which he had already placed on the bed is what is already known to him as a very old and somewhat dangerous one; 'The Nine Doors to the Domain of Darkness', as he was instructed, it must be utterly and completely destroyed.

He sits down with both books, and quickly scans the Vampire one taking note of the strange spelling of the word Vampire, after he looks through it, realizing it's just a short silly fictional romance story, he flips it onto the bed, then places the other on his lap and slowly opens this 'Nine Doors' Novel, he being very fluent in Latin he begins to read some of it. After reading a few pages he closes it and thinks,

To me, it's mostly just devil-worshiper gibberish, so as instructed I will destroy it later this evening, after I have my dinner at the nearby 'Horseman Tavern'.

Victor returns to the room after being out on the Hudson River bank hunting an animal for a quick Blood feeding, he finds that Rachael is in the bathroom, and he looks for the book Mystic Vampyres, which she wrote as Mia Harkness, not finding it where he believed he had left it, he goes to the closet to get another copy and a bookmark, taking the box down from the shelf and lying it on the bed he notices something he had not seen before, what looks to be a rather strange looking large coin, takes it out of the box along with a copy of the book and a bookmark. Puts them all on the night table, and puts the box back where it was in the closet. He will ask Rachael about this coin when she is finished with her bathing and comes out from the bathroom.

U.S. Marshal Michael, now back in his room after having his dinner, takes a flashlight from his bag and the novel '*The Nine Doors*' from the bed where he had left it and heads down to the Hudson River, on his way there he crosses paths with Victor, coming the other way, they pass one another simultaneously say good evening, to each other and keep walking in their opposite directions.

After walking along the River for a while Michael comes to a small clearing and feels this will be a good place to destroy the Novel by burning it, with his foot he clears a spot close to the water of any flammable items, like you would to make a campfire. He kneels down and opens the novel quickly tears out the pages piling them up on the cover, from his pocket takes out a lighter ignites the pile, and watches it burn, it procures a thick black smoke the flames begin to spark, and in a flash, the novel is now a pile of black ashes, with a good size fallen branch he moves it all into the River. Satisfied with this task being completed he stands up brushing away any soil and debris from his slacks, and starts slowly walking in the direction of heading back to his room, suddenly from the corner of his eye, he believes he sees a shimmering figure far off among the dense trees. He hesitates for a few moments just observing where he saw it, after waiting for a moment, it does not reappear again, so he continues on his way back to his room.

Victor shakes his head as he stands looking out the window of their room overlooking the River, thinking,

Did I really see a lustrous figure of a person out among the trees or did I just imagine it, and should I mention it to Rachael?

He moves away from the window to sit in the chair next to it, with the book Mystic Vampyres in his lap and the large coin on top of it. Rachael comes out of the bathroom rubbing her hair to dry it. Victor asks,

"How was your bath, dear?"

"It was fine. Did you find what you needed out along the Riverbank?"

"Yes I did, and I do feel much better now! There are a couple of things I'd like to ask of you."

"Yes, my love, you may ask of me anything you'd like."

"Maybe you should sit down first."

"Oh, you wanting me to sit, it must be some things rather serious."

She sits at the desk and wraps the towel around her head asking,

"Ok, Victor, what is troubling you, my sweet? Please pray tell."

"First, I came back and couldn't find my copy of your novel where I had left it, so I procured another from the box on the shelf in the closet and found this."

He holds up the coin.

"Oh, that old thing, was my dad's, I found it in the desk drawer in the Library at the Cliff House in Mystic, it was most likely his granddad Romeos'. It is a two-faced Janus coin, and it's very old, its meaning is that a person has two sides to them like he did and we now have. I keep it as a remembrance of my dad."

"Okay, I was just curious about it."

"So, my love, what is the other thing you wanted to talk to me about?"

"Well, while I was out on the Riverbank just after I had finished my Blood feeding, and had put the now dead animal's body into the River, I stood up and looked around and saw something rather strange off in the dense trees."

Victor stops talking and lowers his head. Rachael waits a moment then stands to move closer to him sensing that he's having trouble telling her, taking one of his hands in hers she squats down, looks up a him, and gently asks.

"Victor, please, what is it you thought you saw?"

Looking into her eyes he begins,

"Well, this will sound crazy, but I believe I saw a glowing translucent ghostly figure of a man moving among the trees."

"A man! Are you sure it was a man?" "Rachael, that's what it looked like to me."

She stands and thinks,

Could it be, could it possibly be the Spirit of my father?

3.

Rachael Wakes Early, just before sunrise starts, slowly and ever so gently gets herself out of bed in an effort not to wake Victor. Takes what clothing she needs into the bathroom and dresses to go out into the wooded Hudson Riverbank, her curiosity about what Victor told her of what he saw out there has the better of her, and she must investigate his incident for herself.

She hopes in her heart, that the Spirit of her late father, Michael Valli, has returned and is looking to communicate with her once again, like the night when she broke into the Cliff House back in Mystic some years ago, when her Godmother Marlena Varlino lived there.

Dressed now to go, she slowly opens the room door and closes it gently, heads down the side stairway, and goes out the side door of the Riverside Bed and Breakfast so as not to be seen by Mike or Ben in the front lobby, then makes her way to the Riverbank as quickly as she can, and heads to the clearing that she knows so well. With the full Moon still in the sky, which gives her enough light to see without bringing out her Vampire night vision, she stands leaning against a tree and watches and listens, thinking, practically praying,

Oh please, dear father appear to me.

At that precise moment, she believes she sees someone moving within the far-off trees, so she starts to walk slowly toward the area, coming to another clearing, but this one is rather strange to her, at the opposite end of it two trees standing side by side form an arch with their thick lower branches, like bending to someone's will, suddenly an oval of golden light appears within the arch, she takes a step back, and abruptly a voice, familiar to her inserts into her mind,

'*Rachael, my Child be not afraid, it is me, the Spirit of your father.*'

She goes down on one knee and nervously answers out loud,

"I am not afraid just very much pleasantly surprised. Ha, ho, how, I, I mean how are you here and why, father?"

'Well, my dear, as you may know, my little secret friend and your childhood friend Gabrielle Varlino was killed by a drunk driver at 10 years old, her spirit appeared to me in the attic and helped me to crossover into the white light, the light you see me in now is golden, this is a returning light and also allows me to communicate with you in your mind. Generally, a deceased person may not return, but I struck a bargain with the 'powers that be' to allow me to see and converse with you.'

"You did this for me! I would surmise that you have something rather important to speak to me about, then."

'Yes, I do. I know what has been happening to you since my departure, you want to have love in your life, just as I once did, with your mother, but it didn't work out that way, I believe you know what happened, so I'll not hash it over again.'

"Yes Father, I know of all you have said so far, so tell me why you have come to me now, please."

'I do know what you want to do with Victor, I would advise against it.'

"I take it, you are talking about me wanting to have children with him."

'Yes, and like I already said to you, I will warn you against doing this.'

"Why not father? I just want to have a family."

'My dear child, I understand and feel your wants, but it would be a Family of Vampire!'

"Yes, father. What else would two people like me and Victor produce?"

'I am telling you, not to even attempt doing this, please.'

"Father, I have the love of Victor, now I want the love of a family!"

'Well, my child, just do me one thing, please.'

"And what is that father?"

'Give it some more thought, please!'

"I will do that much for you, but I can not promise you, that I will not try to have a family."

Michael Valli's ethereal image starts to fade within the golden light.

Rachael reaches out to him and pleads,

"Father oh my dear father, please don't leave me now!"

'My sweet child Rachael, I have no control over the time they allowed me to appear to you, if I can, I will return to speak with you again.'

Rachael rises from her kneeling position and with her face in her hands she weeps, and through her tears, she softly says aloud,

"Oh my dear father, I will think about what you advised of me, and I will seriously consider it. I will promise you that much."

She shifts and wipes her clothing to clear away any debris from her knee and her apparel. Watching in amazement as the two branches move back to how they naturally would be. The sun is now beginning to rise in the sky on a new day, so she begins to make her way back to the Inn, wondering,

Should I tell Victor about this encounter with my father's Spirit? He may think I just dreamt it or have just lost my mind, and if he does, so be it. So I'll take the day and think about it. After all, it is said, 'fools rush in where angels fear to tread', and by no means am I an Angel.

She enters the side door the same way she had left the Riverside B&B Inn, then up the side stairway, and makes her way quietly back to her room, entering softly to happily find, Victor still in bed asleep, she goes into the bathroom and quietly changes back into her sleeping attire that she had left in there, then quits the bathroom, placing her folded street clothing on the desk chair, like she normally would, then gently gets back into bed. Victor feeling her movement, reaches over to bring her close, to spoon with him. She breathes a sigh of relief, closes her eyes, and falls off to sleep with a knowing smile on her face.

4.

Rachael And Victor rise and get dressed to go down to breakfast. At their table, Victor observes that Rachael is barely eating or drinking any of her breakfast. Benjamin, who is working the breakfast hour, filling water glasses and topping up hot coffee cups. He leans into her respectfully and softly asks of Rachael,

"Is there anything wrong with your food, you barely touched it. Are you feeling ill?"

"No, Ben I am not ill, just not very hungry this morning, is all, but thanks for your concern."

"No prob, Rachael."

He straightens up looks at Victor and asks,

"Victor, would you like a top-up of your coffee?"

"Yes please, thanks, Benjamin."

After Ben walks away, to the next table.

Victor leans in close to Rachael and softly asks, in her ear,

"Rachael are you all right, is there something troubling you?"

"Yes, Victor, a few things are bothering me, but now is not the time or the place to discuss them. Later, please."

"Okay, Rachael you will tell me later. Right?"

"Yes, maybe, my love, after you finish your breakfast, I'd like for us to take a stroll along the River and we can talk then. Okay?"

"Yes my dear, yes, by all means, my love. Wait, maybe?"

She does not answer him, just gives him a loving look.

He lowers his head and finishes his food.

As they stroll together on the wooded Riverbank, and come to the small clearing they both are familiar with, Rachael hesitates for a moment, just looking off into the distance where the trees become very dense, she can't see another clearing that was there earlier, Victor takes her hand in his, sensing a disquiet in her. They continue to walk, now hand in hand, after about fifteen steps, she suddenly stops and looks around.

Victor asks of her,

"My dear, is there something wrong?"

"Well there was a, oh never mind, it's just that I thought there was another clearing right about here."

"I never noticed a second clearing along the bank, maybe further up ahead, maybe? But there is a brook we will come to soon."

She looks around and sure enough, spots the twin trees, where the two branches moved together to form an arch, she thinks,

There was a clearing here earlier, I just know there was, but it's not here now. Strange.

Victor breaks the eerie silence,

"Racheal you were going to tell me, why you were acting a little strange at breakfast."

"Yes Victor, but I fear you will not believe what I have to say."

"Why should I not believe you?"

"Because what I have to tell you will sound a little crazy!"

Victor gently squeezes her hand and looks down at her saying,

"If you feel that I will not believe you, then maybe you should keep it to yourself a little longer, and tell me when you are feeling a little more confident about revealing it to me."

"Yes, I think that would be best for us both."

U.S. Marshal Micheal Aggelos sits in this room at the Ichabod Crain Inn after eating his breakfast that room service has delivered. While finishing his coffee, his cell phone sounds off for a text message. Checking it. He sees that it is a text from the U.S. Marshals Department asking him to call Director Hughs, ASAP. He puts his mug of coffee down and calls in.

The main desk answers his call,

"Hello, U.S. Marshals Department, Main Office. How may I direct your call?"

"Yes, this here is Special Agent Michael Aggelos calling for Director Hughs, please."

"Yes, I believe he is expecting your call, please hold."

Within a moment Director Hughs answers the call,

"Hello, Michael, thanks for getting back to me so soon, I have received a call from the New Orleans Police Department requesting assistance on what they feel is a rather unusual case, and they are not too sure how to handle it so they called us. All I happen to know right now is, that it is in the French Quarter of the City, I will e-mail you any further details, so when you meet their Police Captain, you will have some idea of their problem. Please make your way to the JFK International Airport in New York, I believe you are still in the upper state. Right? Our Jet will be awaiting your arrival, to take you to the New Orleans Airport."

"Yes, Director Sir, am just about finished up here with my private matters. Will get to the Airport, right quick! And as usual will report back to ya when I am finished with this hear case."

"Good, be looking forward to your report."

"Yup, Director Sir, bye for now."

"Yes Michael, good luck! Bye."

Rachael and Victor step out of the wooded Riverbank and onto the road, making their way back in the direction of the Riverside B&B Inn. Suddenly Victor stops and turns her to him,

"Rachael there is something I want to ask of you."

She questioningly looks up at him,

"What is it, my love?"

"Mike's brother Peter, you know, the owner of Pete's garage and gas station up on Main Street, has rebuilt a classic Harley Davidson, and I would like to buy it for us. What do ya say?"

"Well, what can I say?"

"Rachael, you could, please say, yes, my love, if it will make you happy Victor, then okay you should buy it. And, I really would love, for us to take a day trip Cycle ride, up to that riverside restaurant we went to a while ago and had those delicious ribs. Remember? Then on up to Bear Mountain."

"Yes, Victor that sounds very nice."

"Okay, great, when we get back to the Inn, I'll go up to Pete's place and tell him I will buy it! You'll see, it will be a fun little trip for us."

She smiles up at him, giving him an agreeing murmur,

"Mmmm."

And they continue walking now at a somewhat faster pace.

Now at the Inn Rachael goes in, while Victor heads up to Pete's garage on Main Street. Inside the lobby, Mike is at the registration desk working, while Ben sits at his station on the Lobby Bench reading a magazine.

Mike looks at her and asks,

"Hey, sweety why the long face and where's Victor?"

"Hi Mike and Ben, he went up to your brother's place to buy the Harley that he rebuilt to buy it, from him."

Ben jumps up from the Bench and excitedly proclaims,

"Wow! That's so bit...!"

Mike quickly gives him a stern look.

So Ben recants with,

"I mean, really cool!"

Racheal looks up at the ceiling and reluctantly adds,

"Yeah, I guess so."

As she starts to walk up the stairs she announces,

"When Vic gets back, please, tell him I'm gone up to lie down."

They both answer her with,

"Sure thing, will do."

Ben sits back down and goes back to reading his magazine, while Mike continues with his work.

U.S. Marshal, Special Agent, Micheal Aggelos checks out of the Ichabod Crain Inn and gets on the road to JFK International Airport in New York City, where he is greeted by the Pilot who informs him that all the clearances have been made, and he now, can as usual, drive his Harley out on the Tarmac to get it loaded onto the Jet's cargo hold so they can get on their way to the City of New Orleans.

Michael now seated in the plane, reads the e-mail from the Director to get what details of the case he has been sent, but the details are only sketchy at best, the only thing he is getting that he can use is the name of the Police Captain which is Captain Stoner, at the Sixth Police Precinct on Front Street in the French Quarter of the City of New Orleans, having all the memories of Agent Angel Seraph, of where she had lived in a condo in Baton Rouge, he has her knowledge of the City of New Orleans.

The U.S. Marshal Jet lands at the Louis Armstrong New Orleans International Airport, and like always Agent Michael waits on the Tarmac for the cargo compartment to be opened to get his Harley out so he can get to the Police Station for his prearranged meeting with Captain Stoner, to get the latest details of the case. He drives the Motorcycle down the ramp and out onto the Tarmac, stops to thank the Pilot, and then makes his way off the runway, onto the street heading in the direction of the City and the Police Station. As soon as he arrives at the station and parks the Bike in their lot, he makes his way to the front door, enters, walks to the front desk, and announces himself to the desk Sargent, immediately the officer calls his Captain to inform him that, the U.S. Marshal he has been expecting has arrived.

5.

Now At The, New Orleans Police Station, Captain Stoner appears at the front desk with his hand out, and greets U.S. Marshal, Special Agent, Michael Aggelos, as they firmly shake hands, he declares,

"Good evenin', Special Agent Aggelos, real good to have you aboard. Might we get you anythin'?"

"A cup a Coffee, with cream, and two sugas would do me just fine, please."

The Captain turns to the desk Sargent, strictly requesting,

"Officer y'all heard the man, bring it to my Office. My Office is right down this way, please do follow me, Marshal."

In the Captain's Office, the Captain gestures for Michael to have a seat. As Michael sits he queries,

"Well, I do understands ya'll have yourselves a real peculiar case here, that you are not too sure hows to handle it, let me assure y'all Captin, that I have handled some of the strangest cases the U.S. Marshals have been asked to assist with, and seeins' as I live in Baton Rouge I am very much familiar with your City and the strange things that can goes on here. What I needs is an update of the problem."

The Captain hands him a File folder, and declares,

"Here's all we have of the case, fer now."

Michael takes the folder, opens it, and gives it a quick scan, he suddenly stops reading, and looks up at the Captain proclaiming,

"A Warlock!"

"Yup, so he claims to be."

"Well, it's a new one for me, still I do very much believes I can handles it for y'all."

At that moment a soft knocking sounds on the Captain's Office door. The Captain responds to it,

"Yes, come in."

It's an Officer with the Coffee for Agent Michael Aggelos, that he requested, Michael stands and takes it, saying,

"Thanks ya kindly, Officer."

And sits back down,

"I sees his address is in this here report of yourn and it points out that it's a purple house in the French Quarter of the City, well iffin' it's not too late, I'd likes to go and sees him right away."

"Well, I don't believes it is too late, my people that patrol that area tells me his house lights are often still on, late into the night."

Michael finishes his Coffee, stands, puts his empty cup on the Captain's desk, and declares,

"Okay then, thanks ya'll for the Coffee, I just figures I'll just be just takens me a ride by his place and haves me a look-see for myself, iffin' you don't have any objection."

"Not at all Marshal, iffins' you feels that you needs any assistance from my Police Officers, y'all just gives us a call asap."

"I don't believes I'll be a needin' any, but thanks y'all anyway."

With that said, Michael quickly quits the Captain's Office, heads out the Police Station's front door then goes promptly to the Parking lot where his Harley is parked.

As he rides to the address of this purple house, he goes over what he did read in the case file reflecting,

It occurs to me, that this is somewhat like the case I was sent on, as Angel Seraph, up there in Salem, Massachusetts a while back, that came to just issuing a cease and desist order, this one just might be as simple as that, but I know never to underestimate a suspect.

Victor enters the Lobby of the Riverside B&B Inn. Mike looks up from this paperwork to greet him,

"So Victor, how did it go?"

"How did what go, Mike?"

"Are you buying my Brothers Classic Harley or what?"

At that, Ben puts down his magazine. Quickly stands up and anxiously inquires,

"Yeah, are ya buying it?"

"Hold on a minute. How did you two know about me deciding on, purchasing the Harley that your brother Pete has...Wait...Rachael must have said something to you two."

"Yup, she did, and then went up to lie down."

Ben chimes in,

"Yup, Victor, she told us to tell you that."

"Oh she did, did she!"

Mike answers him,

"Yes, Victor she did."

"Do you two, do whatever Rachael tells you to do?"

Ben looks over to Mike, as Mike puts up one finger to Ben as a gesture for him to be quiet and then replies to Victor,

"Well Victor we do like her, and we are just trying to be helpful."

As Victor ascends the stairs he replies to them both with,

"Okay, sorry, thanks for trying to be helpful, I guess."

Mike shakes his head and goes back to his work, Ben sits back down and returns to reading his magazine.

Victor unlocks and enters their room to find Rachael asleep on the bed, not wanting to wake her, quietly he sits at the desk and opens the Laptop Computer and it opens to the last web page looked at, which he believes Rachael must have been checking out, to his distress it is a page about miscarriages, he puts his head down into his hands, and thinks sadly,

Oh man, this must be what she didn't want to tell me about.

Not changing the page he slowly closes the Laptop. Turns in the chair to look at where Rachael is on the bed, she rolls over and opens her eyes to see him, and says

"Victor, did you get to talk to Pete?"

He walks over and sits on the edge of the bed, putting his hand lovingly on her shoulder saying,

"Yes, my dear I did, but if you don't want me to buy it, I won't."

"No, Victor if you really want it, then please get it, I just want you to be happy."

He leans into her to kiss her on the forehead and asks,

"Are you hungry?"

"I guess I could eat a little something. And Vic I have noticed you look a little pale. Do you need a Blood feeding?"

"I think so, I'll go out later to find an animal along the Riverbank. After I get you fed. So tell me, what is it you want and I'll go down and get it for you, I'll be room service instead of Ben this time. Might be they have some of that tomato soup you like, so much!"

"That would be great, thanks!"

"Okay, I'll be right back, don't you move a muscle."

Giving her shoulder a gentle squeeze, he rises to leave the room. As he closes the door gently, she rolls over letting out a deep sorrowful sigh and thinking,

Just might be my father's spirit, happens to be right about us not having children.

6.

Now In The Dining room, Victor watches as Ben is doing setups for the evening meal, Ben spots him in the room, and stops working to walk over to him asking,

"Hey, Victor you need something?"

"Yup, my boy I do, would there happen to be any of Jeannes' tomato soup?"

"Give me a moment to find out for you."

"Oh Ben, it's not for me, it's for Rachael."

Ben suddenly stops short and turns around to Victor, proclaiming,

"Oh, then I will definitely see what I can do!"

"Good," Victor replies, and thinks,

For her, the kid would go to the ends of the Earth, I'm sure.

Ben returns quickly smiling to address Victor,

"Well, it's not on tonight's menu but Jeannie told me she has a small amount that she can reheat for you, I mean Rachael. Can I get you anything while you wait?"

"I guess a cup of coffee would be nice, you do know how I like it, I'll be out in the Lobby talking with Mike."

"Okay, I sure do, big guy, I'll bring it out to you there."

Victor walks through the archway, that separates the Lobby from the dining area, he spies Ben's Cycle magazine on the bench and sits down to look at it.

Mike stops what he is doing, to ask Victor,

"So are you going to buy the Harley?"

"I think so, no I know so, yes, I'm going to buy it!"

"Victor you don't sound too sure. Is there a problem with Rachael approving of you getting it?"

"No Mike no problem, no problem at all."

"Okay good. Did you tell my brother Pete that you definitely want it?"

"Well, I told him I would think about it."

"You had better let him know soon because I know of a few other guys in town who were looking at it, I could call him at home right now for you, and you can tell him you want it."

"Would you? Thanks that would be great!"

Mike picks up the house phone and dials his brother Pete's home number, Pete's wife Anna Beth answers the phone,

"Hello?"

"Hi, Anna Beth, it's Mike. How are you feeling?"

"Thanks, your so sweet for askin', Mike, I'm in remission, so I'm feelin' pretty good fer now, hold on I'll get Peter for y'all."

Mike blocks the phone with his hand and says to Victor,

"Pete's wife, I just love her Southern Accent."

"She's from down South I take it."

"You take it right, Mobile, Alabama I believe."

"Hey brother, what's up?"

"I'm calling for Victor he wants to tell you about buying the Bike."

"Does he want to buy it?"

"I'll let him tell you himself."

And hands the phone to Victor.

"Pete?"

"Yup, Victor you want the Bike?"

"I sure do! The price you quoted still stands, right?"

"Yup, sure does, have it ready for you tomorrow. Or is that too soon?"

"No no that's just fine, see you tomorrow!"

He hands the phone back to Mike who hangs it up.

At that moment Ben shows up with the coffee for Victor, he takes it and thanks the kid. Mike chimes in with,

"Hey, Ben where's mine?"

"Coming right up Boss! I'll bring it out with the tomato soup I'm getting for Racheal. Okay, Victor?"

"Yes, my Boy, that's great!"

"Mike looks at Victor and queries,

"Tomato soup for Rachael?"

"Yup, Mike she ain't feeling so hot, so I'm playing room service for her. Tell you why later. Okay?"

Ben brings out the coffee for Mike, and the soup for Rachael, and distributes them accordingly.

Victor takes the soup from him, then thanks Ben as he ascends the stairs back to their room.

U.S. Marshal, Special Agent, Michael pulls his Harley over to a darkened place on the road, where he can see into the interior lighted large room of the purple house of this self-professed Warlock. Leaning against his Bike's seat, he watches for a while, what he can see is, the person in question dressed rather strangely putting on, what looks like a show for an audience, that he cannot see from his vantage point, he decides to walk around the house to see if he can see through other windows who these spectators could be.

As he slowly and quietly walks to the side of the house he can hear voices, of what sounds like to him, to be young girls giggling and laughing. As he keeps walking to the back of the house he takes notice of a back door leading out to a back street. He takes note that this could be an easy escape option, he will need someone to cover the back. If and when he confronts this person.

Making his way back to the road, he quietly walks his Harley away from this purple house, so that, it will not be heard by anyone in the house, when he starts it up and drives away, back to the Police Station, to arrange for some backup for watching the rear door.

Now back at the Police Station, he explains to the Captain what he needs. The Captain tells him he cannot arrange that for tonight, so it would have to be tomorrow night. He tells the Captain that he will need a place to spend the night, and the Captain offers him the use of one of the empty holding cells toward the back of the building. Michael agrees and goes to get settled in for a night's sleep. But first, he calls, Jake the airplane Pilot to explain the situation and that he will drive himself to his condo in Baton Rouge when this case is completed and he'll just send in his report, so he'll not be needing the U.S. Marshal's Jet Plane, and that he can take off back to Washington DC at his discretion.

7.

Victor Walks Quietly among the trees, in the late afternoon, on the Hudson River bank, stalking an animal quarry for a Blood feeding he requires. As he approaches the well-known clearing, by him and Rachael, suddenly off in the distance, he spies a bright figure moving among the trees. It seems to him that it is the ghostly image of a man, not too sure, he begins to move closer to where it appears to be, and as he does so it seems to, move further away from him. He stops to watch it and thinks,

Strange, as I thought I was getting closer to it, it seemed to be moving further away from me.

As he continues to study it, the glowing seems to slowly be diminishing and then suddenly goes out, as if someone switched off a light. He shakes his head, runs his fingers through his hair, and his need for Blood directs him back to his hunt for it. Moving now to the far side of the clearing in which he had thought, he already had, he approaches the small stream where deer often come for water, and sure enough, there is one getting a drink, moving soundlessly downwind of it, he slowly makes his way to it, just close enough to lunge and capture it and quickly take its Blood.

After sliding the deer's dead body into the river he takes time to ponder what just happened with the glowing figure and again he thinks,

It had seemed to me that I was moving through the clearing, but after that glowing thing disappeared I had not moved at all, I was still standing at the beginning of it. Woo, that was really strange, almost as if I was in a dream state.

After clearing away any debris from his clothing, and feeling better for having a Blood-feeding, Victor walks out from the River bank and onto the road heading back to the Riverside B & B, thinking,

I don't believe, I should say anything to Rachael about the strange glowing vision that I saw in the wooded area along the River. She'll probably just think I was hallucinating, and come to think of it. It just could be that I was.

U.S. Marshal, Special Agent Michael Aggelos is awakened in the holding cell that he was given to spend the night in, at the New Orleans Police Station, by an Officer bringing him coffee.

The Officer standing at the open cell door addresses him,

"Good mornin' Sir, I have brung yous a cup of coffee, and when yous is ready our Captin would like to see ya'll. Ya can wash up in the Station's bathroom just down the hallway."

"Thanks, Officer, please be tellin your Captin I'll be in to see him directly."

"Yup, Sir I sures will do that."

"Oh, an Officer thanks for the coffee."

"No prob, Sir."

In the Captain's office. The Captain explains to Micheal,

"I can have a car with two of my Officers available to you tonight. Is that okay with ya?"

"As I told y'all, I will be a needins' them to be at the back door of the purple house to apprehend anyone who comes out that way and holds 'em for questioning. I will radio 'em when I'm attempting to go in. Will that be okay with y'all, Sir?"

"That will be just fine, Marshal. We's is glad to haves y'all on the case."

"Happy to be of help to y'all and your fine Officers, Sir. And Captin, I'm a thinkins I should be able to wrap this up fir y'all tonight."

"I have no doubts about that."

Marshal Michael leaves the Police Station to get himself some breakfast at the nearest Waffle House Restaurant. While the U.S. Marshal finishing his coffee from his breakfast his cell phone rings, he answers it,

"Hello?"

"Marshal, where y'all at? I meant to gives y'all a portable radio."

Michael enlightens him of his whereabouts, so the Captain informs him.

"Okay, Marshal my Officers will gives y'all the radio to call'em when you needs 'em. I'll sends 'em to y'all pronto." After a short interval, he continues with,

"My Officers are now on their way to y'all location."

After receiving the radio from the Officers they leave him, stating,

"Catch yous later, Sir."

He responds in the positive, as they leave him.

Later that evening, Michael parks his Harley across the street from this purple house and watches and listens for a while. After a few minutes, he once again hears the giggling for what sounds to him to be young girls. He decides to attempt entry to this abode, before he walks to the front door, he quietly informs the Officers with the radio they gave him, they softly answer him with,

"Roger!"

He then knocks hard on the door. From within he hears a man's voice,

"Coming, just a moment, please."

at the same time, he hears this man instructing,

"Quickly now girls, go out the back way."

The two Officers at the back of the house, standing outside their patrol car move quickly to the girls and stop them, saying,

"Okay, young ladies get in the car, now!"

Immediately they do as they are instructed without a sound.

On the portable radio, the Officers quietly inform Michael that they have the girls in custody.

At the front door, it finally opens to reveal a man wearing what looks to be a long purple dressing gown with strange-looking graphics adorning it. He asks politely,

"How may I help you?"

Showing him his badge he announces,

"I am U.S. Marshal, Special Agent Michael Aggelos, I would like to come in and speak with ya'll."

This strangely dressed man moves aside saying,

"Certainly Marshal, come on through,!"

As Michael enters the house he asks,

"Just what is goins' on in here?"

"Oh, please let me assure you, nothing unlawful!"

"Well, let me assure ya'll, two local Police Officers have right at this very moment apprehended some young girls, now in their patrol car that had come out the backway of this very of yourn house, in which I did hear ya'll tell them to do so. So let me inform you, of the laws about entertaining underage girls, it is not a proper thins' to do and ya'll, can be prosecuted fir doing so. Do you clearly understand me? And if ya'll continue with this behavior, ya'll fir sure can be apprehended and go to trial as a pedophile."

"Oh, Marshal, please, let me assure you, nothing of the like, is happening here!"

"I would strongly suggest that ya'll stop whatever is goins' on here immediately and that you be issued a *cease and desist* order, by tomorrow, and I personally, will insist and endorse it to the Police Captin. The local Police will be keepin' an eye on ya'll."

"Yes Sir, thank you, Sir."

With that Michael quits this purple house, walking to his Bike he thinks, after informing the Officers of what to do about this incident,

I am glad of the way this turned out, not at all, disappointed at the outcome, and now to get home.

He starts his Harley and heads off in the direction home in the city of Baton Rouge.

Victor enters the B & B lobby, hearing the door chime, Mike lifts his head from his paperwork, greets him, and questions,

"Good evening Victor. You gonna buy the Harley from my brother Pete tomorrow?"

"Yup Mike, I sure am!"

"Good."

As he responds to Mike's query, he heads upstairs, to his and Rachaels' room.

8.

Victor Walks Into their room and not seeing Rachael he calls out for her,

"Rachael?"

She answers him from inside the bathroom,

"Victor, I'm in the bathroom, be out in a minute."

He sits at the desk and notices that her laptop is on, showing the screensaver, he is relieved that the page about having a miscarriage, that he saw before, was not up. He reflects,

Should I ask her why she was on that Internet page? If I do it will need to be with a caring attitude, very caring and understanding.

Racheal comes out from the bathroom drying her hands on a towel, sits in the chair by the window, and asks him,

"Victor, my love, are you going to buy the Harley later today?"

He ponders before answering her,

Not always a good thing, when she adds 'my love' to her statements or inquiries.

"Yes, my dear, I am and he also has two helmets a black one and a purple one, that are included in the price. Did you not tell me you had a purple one when you rode your Scooter when you lived in Mystic?"

"Yes, I did, how sweet of you to remember that. My real Dad's mother, my Grandmother Carmella, my Me-Ma, I affectionately called her, gave it to me for my sixteenth birthday."

"Didn't she also give you the Cliff House?"

"Yes, that was for my High School graduation gift. She was the sweetest Lady, I do miss her, and my mom, also. But like I told you I had to leave, things seemed to be getting too hot there, and I was afraid the authorities would approach me, with questions that I couldn't give truthful answers to. And besides my mom was beginning to get on my case."

"How long do you think we can stay here before things get like that, or you start to feel the same way?"

"Victor that is not an easy question to answer right now, we will need to wait and see how things go around here. Just please, remember to only use people for a Blood Passion feeding who are passing through the area."

"Something that has been rolling around in my mind is. Whatever happened to Angel?"

She answers him somewhat irately,

"What! Why are you wondering about her? You do remember she tried to kill me, right? She tried to kill, the woman you now, love! She's gone. And I for one, am glad that she is, saves me the trouble of getting rid of her myself. With the help, I was expecting from you."

"Please, Rach, please, don't get upset with me, I was just wondering what happened to her and also who is this Michael person that seems to have taken her place, I mean everyone around here looks at him like they know him in the way they knew her. Don't you think that is a little weird that we do not see him the same way as they do?"

She looks out the window at the River, before answering him,

"Yes, of course, I do, but that's a problem for another time."

"My love, is there a problem for now?"

"Why, whatever do you mean?"

He walks over to her where she is sitting at the window, he goes down on one knee, gently takes her hand, looks up at her, and calmly states and asks,

"Sweetheart, I happened to notice you had an internet page up on your Laptop recently about miscarriages. Is there something I should know about that you can tell me?"

"Well, Victor, oh Victor sweetheart, I thought I was pregnant, but when my monthly visitor did come, I was afraid I was having, what I thought was, a miscarriage. But my love, what it was, was just my regular monthly visitor, so after that, I went online to learn about miscarriages. I will get some pregnancy test things next time I'm up on Main Street and go to the drug store and get some, so this shall not happen again to us."

She gently puts for hand on the back of his head and lovingly implies.

"Oh Sweetheart, you were worried about me, I'm so sorry that you saw that page on my Laptop, so if something like this should ever happen again, I will tell you right away, but I don't believe that it will if I have the tests."

He slowly lifts his head, looks into her eyes, and replies,

"I am very sorry that I jumped to the wrong conclusion, that will never happen again either, it's just because I do love you so much and was concerned about you. Sorry!"

"Victor my love, you never have to be sorry about being concerned about me and my feelings, I am a strong woman. And yes I had to be because I had resigned myself to being on my own until I met you, that is. I am still getting adjusted to having someone like you, in my life, and now not being alone in what was my unique plight."

"Okay then if that is just about cleared up. I'll need to go up to Pete's to pay him for the Harley and then later we can start planning our trip to Bear Mountain for tomorrow."

Racheal answers him somewhat dispassionately,

"Yup, I can't wait."

Victor stands and heads for their room door, stops turns to her, and says, excitedly,

"I'll be back directly, with the bike and the two helmets! I love you!"

"Okay, Victor, I'm sure I'll hear you coming!"

"I'm pretty sure, you will."

"Victor, I actually believe, everyone nearby will!"

She proclaims, and he's quickly out the door.

U.S. Marshal Special Agent, Michael Aggelos opens the door to the Condo in the city of Baton Rouge which is now his home. The same home that once was Angels'. He goes right to the Refrigerator to get himself a Beer, takes a long swallow, and proclaims,

"Mmmm. Long time, since I've tasted this earthly delight!"

Now at the Desktop Computer, he turns it on to make out his report and send it into the Washington DC Marshal's Central Office and a copy to the Police Captain of New Orleans. As he sits back and takes another swallow of the Beer he thinks,

My first big mission is done, so this is what Angel was doing, and getting paid for it. Quite simply I'd have to say, maybe there will be something much more exciting and challenging coming up soon, I hope. In the meantime, I really should get a Laptop Computer. Yup, tomorrow after I get a good rest now. That Cot in the New Orleans Police Station holding cell was not at all comfortable, the bed here better be, or I'll just have ta' get a new one. And thinking about my next mission really would like one with a battle to it, yup, always enjoyed myself a good fight.

With that final thought, he falls off to sleep.

Michael wakes after his much-needed restful nap, now sitting in the living room with a freshly brewed mug of coffee, he calls into the Washington DC Central Marshals' Office,

"Hello, this is the Washington DC Marshals Office. How may I direct your call?"

"Yes, ma'am, this here is Special Agent Michael Aggelos, Lookins' to speak with Director Hughs."

"Director Hughs is in a meeting. Would you care to wait, Sir?"

"Yes, thanks y'all kindly ma'am."

He puts his phone on speaker mode, placing it down beside him on the couch, just as he raises his mug to his lips a female voice on the phone questions,

"Hello Sir, are you there?"

"Yup, I's here!"

"The Director is now available for to speak with you."

"Alrighty good, puts me through to him, please."

"Hello, Agent Aggelos, your report looks good as usual. What can I do for you?"

"It's ain't anythin' you can do fir me, Sir. I is ah calling to see inffin there be anythin' I can do fir you, Director."

"Well, let me see here, can you hold on for a moment and I'll check."

"Sure thin' Sir."

After a short interval, the Director returns with

"Hello, agent?"

"Right here, Sir."

"We did get a call from the Police Captain, right there in your city of Baton Rouge, she says something about a VooDoo Queen causing what she called, 'ah mêlée in the City Center.

Michael, just let me get some more intel on this and I'll get back to you if this Police Captain feels that they need some help with this."

"Okay, Sir, be right here iffin yous would be ah needins' me. So long."

With that said, they both hang up from the call.

9.

Victor Wakes At nine AM and is rather anxious to get on the road to Bear Mountain, so without waking Rachael he rushes off in her car to the DMV to register the Harley for their road trip. Rushing back to the Riverside Bed and Breakfast Inn, he goes in to ask Mike for a screwdriver to attach the license plate to the Bike, Mike gives him one from his registering counter drawer. He thanks him, but before he can leave to use it, Mike stops him to inform him,

"Victor, Rachael is in the dining room having her breakfast."

"All right, Mike good, tell her what I'm doing, and that I'll be in to have mine with her directly."

"Okay, Victor will do."

Now finished installing the plate on the Bike he enters the dining room, spots Rachael, slides into the chair next to her, and announces,

"Rach, the Bike is ready to go, we can get on the road just as soon as you are ready to go!"

"Yes, Victor, Mike informed me of what you were doing, I can be ready just as soon as I finish my meal, then I'll get dressed for the ride, and you, my love, should have something while you wait for me."

Ben, comes to the table addresses and asks Victor,

"Morning Victor. What would you like to eat?"

"Um, Ben, just coffee for me, thanks, I've the Harley ready for our first road trip."

"That is Super! Where you two headed?"

"Up to Bear Mountain, Ben."

"That's so cool it's really nice up there."

"Just thinking, what you gonna do about lunch?"

"Well, was figuring we'd stop and get some food to…"

Racheal cuts him off,

"Victor my sweet, Chef Jeannie is packing us a picnic lunch for our road trip."

"Wow! That's awesome. We can stop somewhere nice and eat by the River."

"Yup, that's just the idea I had for us, I'll grab us a blanket from our room for our Riverside Picnic!"

Ben shows up with a mug for Victor, and a pot of coffee, pours it for Victor, and goes to top up Rachaels but she waves him off. Now finished with her breakfast, she stands up to leave the dining room to go up to their room to make ready to go.

Ben sits in Rachael's' empty chair, states and asks,

"Victor, I haven't really had a good look at your Harley, yet. Is it the red one I caught a glimpse of in the parking lot when I came here this morning for work?"

"Yup, Ben that's her, ain't she a beaut!"

"Before you two leave, I'd love to get a closer look at your Steel Horse."

"Sure thing kid, come on out with me and get yourself a good look-see at her."

As they drew closer to the Harley, Ben begins to get really excited,

"Wow! Victor she really is a sweet Bike, really Boss! He chokes up a little and then continues with a request,

"Victor could I just, I mean would it…would it be okay if I sat on her for a second?"

"Sure kid try her, see what it feels like."

He carefully swings his leg over gets on the seat and politely inquires,

"Maybe when you get back…or possibly you could tomorrow take me for a little ride?"

"Yup, I could do that, but probably tomorrow would be best."

"Okay, tomorrow then Victor, that would be, oh so bitch-in!"

Victor notices Rachael step out the side door of the inn onto the deck. He gives Ben the purple Helmet, asking him to give it to her, and he seats himself on the Bike, and without starting it backs it up to be facing the parking lot exit. Rachael approaches him with her Helmet and asks,

"Why's Ben have such a big smile on his face?"

"I told him I would take him for a ride on the Bike tomorrow."

"Well, that's a ride for him tomorrow, today is a ride for me, I mean for us!"

She puts the package of food in the saddlebag, adorns herself with the purple Helmet, and jumps up behind him, putting her arms around his waist, saying,

"All set back here, let's go!"

Victor pushes the start button and the Bike roars to life, up on the deck Ben quickly turns round and gives them the thumbs-up sign. Shifting into first gear, and throttling up, he stops the Bike at the exit to the street. As he checks to see that the street is clear, Rachael half turns back to Ben and gives him an OK'ing thumbs-up. And with a roaring of the engine, they pull out on the street and are off on their first road trip.

Benjamin stands on the deck watching them go until they are out of his sight, he then goes into the Lobby, where Mike is working behind his registration counter, so he sits on the Lobby Bench with his head lowered, Mike notices this and asks him,

"What has you troubled, Ben?"

"Ah, nothin' Mike," with his head still down hesitating in his thoughts, and suddenly looks up at Mike and continues,

"Well, Mike ya see, it's just that, I just wish that, I mean is I'm just wishing I was old enough to get me a Harley, as Victor did, and now has, it so Bit…

Instantly Mike cuts him off,

"Ben, what have I said to you before about using that word around the Inn?"

"Real sorry Mike, sometimes it just almost slips out."

"Ben you really need to watch that almost slip of the tongue, at least around here, that is. And Ben you'll be old enough, soon enough, for those things to have in your life, don't rush it, Boy."

"Yup, I guess you're right, it's just that sometimes…oh never mind, I'm gonna take a walk."

"Please don't be gone too long, we have some new guests checking in soon, and I'll need you to do your job, showing them to their rooms."

"I'll stay within view of the parking lot, and if I see a car pull in, I'll come right back to do my job."

"Okay good, just don't wander off too far."

"I won't go too far off, Mike."

Victor and Rachael ride for about forty-five minutes, Rachael gently squeezes his shoulder to get his attention. He instantly pulls the bike to the shoulder of the road shuts down the engine, and asks,

"What is it, my dear, is there something wrong?"

"Nothing is wrong my love, I just could use a restroom soon, please!"

As he points to the wooded area he asks,

"Could you make do of right here?"

Slightly irritated she answers him,

"No sweetheart I need a lady's room!"

"Okay okay, next place I see I'll pull in for you."

"Please, try to make it soon."

"Yup, will do."

So with that said he starts up the Bike and gets back on the road. In less than a minute he pulls into a place where he believes has a restroom for her to use. She jumps off the Bike, removes and hands him her Helmet, and runs inside. He takes off his Helmet, runs his hand through his hair, and waits. She comes out, walks up to him, and says,

"Thank you, sweetheart, I needed that, sorry for getting a little impatient with you."

He gives her a quick kiss and replies,

"That's okay sweetheart, when ya gotta go, ya gotta go!"

They put their Helmets on, she gets back on the Bike and they resume their road trip. Before too long, they come within sight of the Bear Mountain Bridge that crosses over the Hudson River, Victor gets an uneasy feeling as they get closer to it. He abruptly pulls the Bike over just before they can cross over to the other side, and he stops. Rachael reacts with one questioning word,

"Problem?"

"No hun, I'm just getting a little hungry, thought right here on the River bank would be a nice place for us to have our picnic. Is that okay with you?"

"Sure if you want to eat, we'll eat, right here!"

They walk down to the Riverbank, with the food and blanket finding a nice place, in the shade of a large tree not far from the arch of the Bridge, where it begins to go over the Hudson River. With the blanket laid out, they sit down to eat. Rachael opens the container of food which has kept it fresh and warm. Victor's back is toward her looking at the River he notes by saying,

"Wow, that food smells really great!"

As Rachael begins to unpack the container of food, from the corner of her eye, she notices a raggedy-looking person come out from up under the Bridge, Victor is still watching the River's current sinuously roll by, so he does not see what she sees, she softly tells him,

"Victor don't be alarmed, just be still, but a very raggedy-looking person has come out from under the Bridge and is slowly coming toward us. I believe it's a homeless man."

Victor stands up to confront this person questioning,

"And who might you be?"

"I, Sir, am nobody."

"You must be somebody. Everyone is someone?"

"I see you two are having yourselves a little picnic meal here on my Riverbank."

Victor replies to this ridiculous statement irately inquisitive,

"Your, Riverbank, what makes this your, Riverbank?"

"Yes, Sir my Riverbank! I live here."

"You, what!"

This man then turns half around and points to where the Bridge begins to cross the River and claims,

"Right up, in there where the Bridge begins is my home, I am called the Troll or just Troll, and I've seen me some strange things, that no one else could have seen."

"And just what is it you have seen, Mr. Troll?"

At this point, Rachael stands up with a Fried Chicken Drumstick, holding it with a napkin, to ask this person,

"I bet you're hungry, yea?"

Troll answers her,

"Yup, I could eat."

"Okay good," With this Drumstick still in the napkin she begins to walk passed him toward the place he pointed out under the Bridge, also she continues to speak to him,

"Why don't you tell me about this strange thing or things you have seen and show me where."

Troll wants the food so he follows her. Victor calls out to Rachael, she puts her hand up to him with one finger meaning to give her a minute. Victor intensely watches them walk away.

   They stop in the shade under the arch. She hands him the food and asks,

"So Mr. Troll, just what is it you have seen here and when?"

He answers her with food in his mouth,

"Not, Mr. Troll, just Troll or the Troll, if you please, Mis."

"Okay Troll, please now, tell me, just what it is you have seen."

He swallows, wipes his mouth on this sleeve, and asks,

"If I tell ya, can I get some more of that Chicken?"

10.

Victor Watches Rachael walking from under the Bear Mountain Bridge, back to their picnic place on the Hudson River Bank. As she draws closer, he stands to ask her,

"What does he want, now?"

"Victor, please, yes he does, and he has something to tell me if we give him more and it sounds to me like he knows that we'd like to know. And we have plenty of food, and besides I could use a feeding, you want in? We could share this one."

"Well, I just had a feeding from an animal recently, but I could use some human blood. And I saw something weird in the wooded Riverbank when I did it, or just before I did it, I wanted to speak with you about it. It really was quite strange."

"Yes, my love, you can tell me all about it, just let me hear what this vagrant has to tell me and we can discuss it then."

Finishing her statement she picks a piece of chicken up and goes back to the Troll, sitting on an empty wooden apple box, as she approaches him as he places another one up for her to sit on saying,

"Please, come into my parlor, and have a seat."

She hands him the food as she sits down, states, and questions,

"Here you go. Now what is it you know that you believe I'd want to know?"

He takes a bite chews it quickly swallows and begins,

"Well I have lived here for some time now and I get to recognize, without being able to see them, by the sound of the different types of vehicles crossing over the Bridge above me."

"So?"

"So, one time something really weird happened, just thought you'd like to hear what it was I saw."

He stops to take another bite of the Chicken.

Rachael begins to get impatient with him, for taking so long to tell her about this weird thing he heard and saw.

"Okay, now, you have the food. Are you going to tell me or not?"

"Oh yes, I was up there," he points up to where the Bridge starts to go over the water or ends depending on your point of view, "just starting to fall asleep when I hears me a large truck, you know like one of those eighteen-wheelers, begin to cross over the Bridge and then I hears a motorcycle coming from the other direction."

He stops to take another bite.

Impatiently she asks,

"Okay and then what happens?"

Still chewing he replies,

"Well, I heard a tire squeal, I think it was the Bike's tire and then a crash of the guardrail breaking, then a large Motorcycle appeared falling towards the River, next thing, unexpectedly this rider jumped off the bike and landed just about right here under my Bridge, where we are sitting now. There wasn't really anything I figured I could do for this person, I just thought they were dead, so I closed my eyes and went to sleep."

He takes another bite.

Rachael irately questions,

"That's it, that's all?"

He swallows hard and says,

"Oh, no, there's more, this is where it gets really strange!"

"Okay do tell, or do you need more food?"

"Yes but, let me tell you first, what happened next."

"By the way, did you notice the color of this Bike?"

"Yup, I only saw it just before it hit the water, but I think, it was purple and black."

Rachaels' eyes widen, and she has a questioning thought,

Could this be what happened to Angel sounds like her Bike, I don't think there are many Harleys with that color scheme.

She reacts to his statement,

"So, purple and black, hah?"

"Yup, I think it was."

"So now, what else is there to this story of yours?"

Another bite, he chews and swallows,

"Oh yeah, I don't know how long I was asleep, but it was still dark when this very bright light woke me, this rider who sounded to me, to be a woman, who was still lying on the ground was pleading with the light or something that was inside it, I couldn't see or hear if there was or not, but she was strongly appealing to it, for her to stay here on Earth, so she said. And then in a flash, she and all she had with her was a cloud of ash and gone just that quickly. Strange don't you think? "

Rachael stood up from the wooden apple carten she was sitting on, waved to Victor to come to her, and stepped around to the back of this Troll person, as he stood up with his back to her, she quickly brought out her Vampire powers wrapping her arms tightly around him, released one of her hands grabbing his hair pulling his head back to the breaking point, and then sinks her fangs deeply into his neck. It all happened so fast, Troll never had any time to say anything at all or make any sound, even if he had there wasn't anyone around to hear it. Just as she is about to finish with this victim, Victor shows up to get his share. When he finishes he carries this now-empty Blood donnors' body to the Rivers' edge and lays him in the water so that the current will take it away.

As they walk together to their picnic spot, Rachael relates all that the Troll had told her, Victor stops short and says,

"I told you I saw what looked to be Bike handlebars moving down the River. Remember?"

"Yes, but at that time we didn't know what we know now."

Rachael adds,

"So now we know that somehow she was replaced with this Michael, U.S. Marshal Agent, but everyone sees him and knows him as Angel. Very strange that we don't, could it be that our brain chemistry is that different than regular people's are?"

"Would have to be the only logical answer, I'd say you have hit on the truth about all this."

Rachael answers him,

"Okay so we've learned something rather important today, I say we clear up and continue on our little road trip."

Victor replies in agreement,

"And I say, great idea, my love!"

11.

U.S. Marshal, Special Agent, Michael Aggelos is relaxing on the deck of the Condo in Baton Rouge, Louisiana, that had been occupied by Angel and Gabriell, which is now his earthly home, reading a book authored by one of his favorite Earthly American authors, Robert E. Howard, when suddenly his cell phone rings. The display shows: that U.S. Marshal Director Hughs' office is calling him, putting in a bookmark and his book down on the small table beside him, he answers the call,

"Hello, this here is U.S. Marshal Aggelos."

A woman's voice replies,

"Yes Sir, please hold for Director Hughs."

The Directors' voice promptly emerges on the call,

"Hello, Michael. How are you? I believe we have an assignment for you, not too far from you. You are at home right?"

"Yes, I am, and I'm good, Thank ya'll, Sir. Where and when?"

"Well, we recently have received a call from the U.S. Marshals branch Office in Houston, Texas, telling me that they could use some special help with a situation they are not too sure how to handle, please if you can go there and meet with them for the details as soon as you can, that would be great."

"Well, Sir, I can leaves here on my Harley in about an hour, so you can lets 'em know, I'm on my way."

"Will do, thanks, and good luck!"

"Yup, and I'll be a callings ya'll when I gets me there."

"Okay good, and like I said best of luck."

The call ends on that note. Michael goes inside to pack his rucksack, for the ride to the Houston location branch Office, and he enters the location into the cellphone for mapping directions, as he's getting ready to go he reflects,

I sure do hope this is something with some action to it, I'm just itching for a good fight ever since I took Angels' place.

Victor and Rachael get back on the road heading across the Bear Mountain Bridge to the other side of the Hudson River, to continue with their road trip, on his newly purchased refurbished classic Harley Davidson Motorcycle. On their way across, they both notice a section of repair to the left side of the Bridge guardrail, she squeezes his shoulder and points to it and he reacts by nodding his head in recognition. As they reach the other side Victor slows down to go South, toward Bear Mountain Park. When they reach the Park, Victor parks the Bike near the public access building to use the restrooms, they both make use of the facilities, Victor is finished first, so he stands at the Bike waiting for Rachael to finish and appear refreshed. As she appears and approaches him, she makes the hand-to-mouth jester for a drink. He opens the Saddlebag and gets out the bottle of wine in a plain paper bag also two plastic wine glasses, so they walk to the back of the building out of sight of anyone. Rachael had retrieved the blanket, so she spread it out under the shade of a large tree and they sat and had a glass of wine.

She covers Victor's hand, with hers and relates,

"So now we know what happened to Angel, but I don't believe we are off the hook, so to speak, if this Michael person has taken her place we will need to be vigilant about him coming for us, especially if he has all her memory of what's been happening between her and us."

"Rachael, now knowing what has happened to her is good, but still a little unsettling for me. I hope you understand why."

She lovingly squeezes his hand and replies,

"I do understand why you feel that way, I have lost a person I believed I was in love with once."

"You're talking about Shane. Right?"

"Yes, I am Victor, I did tell you about him."

"Yes, you did, and I have had no problem with that, at all."

They both finish their glasses of Wine and stand up to get back on their road trip. Victor informs Rachael, that there is a Bridge further to the South for them to cross over to get back to the Sleepy Hollow side of the Hudson River. Victor pulls over to suggest they get back to the Inn, and Rachael agrees. As they come in sight of the Inn, Victor enters the parking lot, they disembark from the Bike, remove the things in the Saddlebag, and head inside. They enter the Inn Lobby and Ben greets them warmly,

"You're back, safe and sound, awesome. So Victor how did she perform for you?"

Victor looks at Rachael, then looks back at Ben and says,

"Oh right, you mean the Harley."

"Yes. What did you think I meant?"

Victor looks down at the floor and answers,

"Um, well, never mind, she operated perfectly well, no problems at all."

"Good, glad to hear that. So you could take me for that ride tomorrow?"

At that instant, Mike enters the Lobby from the archway that gives access to the dining room and takes his place behind his check-in counter,

"Rachael, Victor, good your back, somebody has shown up asking about Rachael."

She looks up at Victor with a concerned expression and inquires,

"What! Mike, who… who is this somebody?"

"Don't you mean, whom is this somebody?"

"Oh, Mike, please, okay whom is this somebody?"

"Just a moment, please."

Mike then looks over to Ben and instructs him to,

"Ben go into the dining room, and inform that person that Rachael is here, now."

Ben as he is instructed, slowly leaves the Lobby for the dining room.

A fervent wave of anxiety washes over Rachael, she quickly takes Victor's hand in hers, affectionately squeezing it, as a physical sign that she's requesting his support, and then lollops into a Lobby chair just behind her. Victor looks down at her gives her an encouraging stare, and supportingly, but gently squeezes her hand in return. The atmosphere, in the Riverside Bed and Breakfast Inn Lobby, is extremely intense for her and Victor, it is almost so thick you could cut it with a knife.

12.

U.S. Marshal, Special Agent, Michael Aggelos arrives at the U.S. Marshal's Branch Offices in Houston, Texas, where he parks his Harley in their parking lot and then proceeds to go inside. At their reception desk, he shows his credentials to identify himself and then explains why he has come, he is respectively requested to take a seat and wait. The reception agent then makes a phone call to the office of their branch Director, James Cooper.

"Sir, I have Agent Aggelos here, waiting to see you."

"Right, I was expectin' 'em, please tell 'em I'll be with him in a moment."

The reception agent relays the message to U.S. Agent Michael and asks,

"Can I get ya'll a cup of coffee or somethin', Sir?"

"Thanks, some coffee would be just grand, cream with two sugas, please."

Before the agent can return with the coffee for Michael, the Director appears in the waiting area, he walks to Michael with his hand out to greet him cordially. Michael stands to receive this welcoming gesture. As they shake hands, Director Cooper invites Michael to his Office,

"So glad you could come, let us go to my office and I'll fill you in on what we have of this case so far."

"Yes Sir, by all means, although your agent just went to get me a cup of coffee."

"When he does not see ya out here in the waiting area he'll know to bring it to my Office."

In the Director's Office, he takes his seat behind his desk and invites Michael to have a seat, he pulls open his middle drawer and takes out a red folder, just as he attempts to hand it to Michael suddenly a knock is heard on the Office door.

"That must be your Coffee," so he instructs, "Enter!"

Benjamin walks slowly thinking, with what seems to be a slightly crazy thought in his head, and he decides he'll do it, gets to the table with this new Guest having a cup of coffee, awaiting to be informed that the person they've come to see has arrived back at the Inn. He stands looking down at this, for him unknown Guest, the individual notices him just standing there, so lowers their cup and looks up at him questioningly,

"Yes?"

"Ms. Rachael Valli is here now in the Inn Lobby, if you could follow me I can announce you to her and everyone that is there with her."

"Announce me?"

"I, well, I mean, like, you know, introduce you to everyone."

The person rises from their chair smiling and softly sniggering and says,

"Introduce me? I'm not royalty, that requires an announcement or introduction, so just lead on young man."

Ben turns round to show this stranger to the archway, with a grin on his face thinking,

This stranger called me a man, well a young man, still cool.

As Ben gets to the beginning of the archway he suddenly stops and turns to this new arrival at the Inn, he leans in close and whispers,

"Tell me your full name, please?"

He's told their name, then puts up his hand in a signal for them to stay where they are out of sight. With a puzzled look, this individual stands at the beginning of the archway just out of sight of anyone in the Lobby.

Young Benjamin swiftly moves into the center of the archway and stands alone there, all in the Lobby are looking at him with mystifying curiosity in their eyes.

He raises his right hand, puts his left out to his side to where the person is standing unseen and he announces,

"Everyone please, your attention, it gives me great pleasure to present to you all," He gestures for this Guest to come to him, and loudly announces,

"Ms Lucy Howard!"

Ben moves over for her to take this center place, Lucy then quickly steps into the center of the archway.

Racheal with great relief and pleasurable surprise leaps from her chair and swiftly closes the short distance to Lucy, giving her a friendly and very affectionate hug and declaring,

"Lucy, oh Lucy, it's so fetch to see you!"

Victor thinks,

And very relieved, that it's a friend, I would have to fathom a guess.

The general tension in the room fades away quickly, and any that may have been feeling it breathe easy, now.

Mike addresses Ben with, "Ben, my Boy, since when have you become such a Showman?"

"Well, Mike the opportunity presented itself, so I played it off. It was fun!"

Mike just laughs and hands the room key to Ben telling him to get her bags from behind his counter and show Lucy to her accommodation.

As Lucy passes by Rachael and Victor, to follow Ben up the stairs to the second floor to her room. She stops on the stairs and proclaims,

"Rachael, you did tell me I should come up here to see you. So I'll meet you and your friend for dinner later?"

"Of course, Lucy we'll both see you then."

Rachael turns to Victor, hugs him, and softly says,

"Oh, Victor," he leans down to hear her, "I thought that it just might be…"

Victor cuts in,

"Rach, I believe I know who you were thinking it might or could have been."

"Yup, I'm oh so glad it turned out to be only, my childhood friend from my hometown of Mystic, Connecticut. I tell ya Victor, I could, so now, use a little nap."

With that said and understood, he escorts her up the stairs to their room so they can both get some rest before they will join Lucy, later for dinner.

13.

U.S. Marshal, Special Agent, Aggelos looks over the report file and looks up to the Director,

"Of course, I'll be a needens' to meet 'em two Officers that have been a working this here case."

"Yup, I'm calling their Captain right now to set up just that."

Director Cooper lifts his desk phone and makes the call, after a short conversation, he hangs up and informs Michael,

"Well that meeting will have ta be latea', they're out on their daily patrol. But he'll set it up with them for latea' when they get in."

"All righty then, I'll get myself checked into my room at that there Courtyard Marriott, in downtown Houston."

"Okay good, I'll have his Officers call you later with the details for ya to meet with 'em."

"Sounds just grand."

"Yup, Agent Michael Aggelos."

With that Michael quits the Office.

He arrives at his Hotel, checks in, and goes to his room, where he cleans up and goes to have a meal in their restaurant. While he's waiting to be served his order, his cell phone rings. He answers this call where this, unknown to him, voice, speaks, questions,

"Might this just be, the U.S. Marshal, Special Agent, Michael Aggelos?"

"Yup, and who might ya'll be?"

"I am Officer James Burgoa, was given your number to call and set up a meeting for us."

"You and your Partner?"

"Yes Sir, myself and my Officer partner, Officer Angela Garcia, We are the two Houston Police Officers that have been working the case and we seem to be getting nowhere with it, this culprit is quite cagey and might I say somewhat dangerous also."

"Okay good. When and where can we meet?"

"Well Sir, our Shift is over at about 2 pm, we could come to you at your hotel and meet then and there if that is okay with you, Sir."

"Yup, that sounds good for me, and Officer, knock off the Sir thing, you both, can address me as Michael."

"Okay, Sir...Um, I mean Michael we will do that, see you later."

"Yes, bye."

Just as the call ends, his meal order arrives.

Lucy arrives in the Inn Lobby slightly early to be seated to eat, seeing the Dining Room still being set up for the meal, she takes a seat in the Lobby. Benjamin enters from the Dining Room and addresses Lucy.

"Hello, we are just finishing doing setups we'll be done soon. May I get you something while you wait?"

"Yup, a cup of Coffee would be just perfect, please."

"Oky doky, will be back in a flash with that, and all the fixings you may need to go with it!"

Just as Ben is coming back into the Lobby with the Coffee for Lucy, Racheal steps on the floor at the bottom of the stairs, and observes Ben come through the archway from the dining room, bringing a tray with Coffee to Lucy, so she follows him to where she is seated.

"Hey, Lucy you came down too early."

"Yup, I did, Rach."

Ben puts the tray down on the small table beside Lucy, turns his attention to Rachael to ask,

"Rachael, may I get you something while you both now are waiting to be seated for the meal? Will there be three of you?"

"Thanks, Ben but I think I'll wait till we are seated, and yes three, Victor should be down directly."

Ben replies,

"I'll see to it that you three get the best table in the dining room."

"Thanks, Ben!"

Lucy interjects,

"He is such a nice young man!"

"Yup, Ben's a sweetie!"

"So Lucy you came up here all by yourself. On the Train, I'd suppose?"

"Oh yes, just me, myself, and I."

"What about... Um?"

"I think you mean Danny?"

"Yes Danny, I remember you mentioned him when I saw you in New York City. Why didn't he come with you?"

"Well, Rach, me and Danny split, not long after you and I had our little chance reunion in the Big Apple."

"Oh sorry."

"Don't be, it was for the best, I've had my eye on someone else anyway and I think he knew it."

Ben enters the lobby to announce that they are beginning seating for dinner, just as Victor shows up at the bottom of the stairs. And he proclaims,

"Well, I'm just in time!"

Rachael and Lucy stand and move over to Victor, Rachael takes his arm. As Ben removes the tray from the table then walks to the archway and says,

"If you would please, follow me to your table."

Now seated by Ben at the front table by the window, he states,

"I'll bring you water and your waitperson will be over with rolls, butter, and menus to take your orders. Please enjoy!"

Rachael appreciatively replies to him,

"Thank you, Benjamin."

With U.S. Marshal Michael Aggelos just about finished with his meal, Houston Police Officers James Burgoa and Angela Garcia show up for their meeting with him. As they approach his table, Officer James Burgoa addresses him,

"Excuse me, Marshal Aggelos, how was your meal?"

"It was good, please both of you sit and have a cup of coffee with me while we talks about this case of yourn, and if you please it's just Michael."

They both have a seat as Michael signals to the waitperson over and is asked to bring a pot of coffee and three cups to the table. They are silent as the coffee is delivered to them and poured, the waitperson leaves them, so they begin to quietly discuss the particulars of this strange case in question.

Officer James Burgoa begins,

"Okay, so first of all, we have been on this case now for only two weeks and we can't seem to obtain much on the comings and goings of this perpetrator who is calling themself Mr. Hyde, plus, we have interviewed any of the victims who were willing to come forward, also the one who was hospitalized after being accosted by this self-styled Mr. Hyde individual, also we have deduced that this Mr. Hyde, is a male, but we could be wrong about that.

14.

U.S. Marshal, Special Agent Michael while sipping his mug of coffee looks over to the Houston Police Officers and inquires,

"So, yeah both been on this here case fir bout two weeks now?"

Officer Burgoa looks at his police partner, and she gives an agreeing nod to him, so he fields Michaels' question,

"Yes Michael, but it has had our constant attention, both of us gathering any and all information bout this culprit."

"Good, so yous should be able ta draw me a map of most, if not all of the locations here in Houston of assaults?"

"Yes we…I mean my partner Officer Garcia has already gone and done that for yeah."

Officer Garcia takes a folded paper from her back pocket and hands it to Michael, he opens it, gives it a good look, looks up at her, smiles then proclaims,

"This here is just whats I be ah needins' to catch this here person calling them selfs Mr. Hyde."

Officer Burgoa asks,

"So Agent, just what might be your first move?"

"I will take the next few days and does' me some covert surveillance of these here locations on your map of downtown Houston, incognito of course. Eventually, I will needins some bait to draw this here person out of hidins'."

Officer Burgoa looks up at Michael and questions him with one word,

"Bait?"

"Yup, James, bait, a lone woman dressed for a night out, standing on the sidewalk, just looking like she is outside her dwelling waiting for an acquaintance to come get her with their car."

James replies,

"But who might be…?"

Michael just points over at Officer Angela Garcia and says,

"She is well-trained in defense, I woulds fathom a belief?"

She answers him sternly,

"Yes, more than just well-trained Agent Michael Sir, I am a committed Marshal artist, as a matter of fact, a 'Champion'!"

"Alrighty then excellent, I'll be in touch, when this there part of this here Mr. Hyde apprehending procedure is ready for ya'll to perform your role in it."

With their initial meeting now somewhat over, the two Offices rise and respectfully take their leave of Agent Michael and the restaurant. Micheal politely signals his server for a top-up of his mug of coffee as he studies the hand-drawn map that Police Officer Angela Garcia has made and given to him.

Rachael, Lucy, and Victor order their meals and cocktails to enjoy while they wait to be served their food orders. Lucy stares out the window just watching the Hudson River roll by on the other side of the Riverside Road. She remarks,

"Rachael you were right about it here, it really is a very lovely location."

"Yes, we like it here just fine. Don't we Victor?"

"Thats right, my dear one, very much, very much indeed."

"Racheal, you really must tell me, how the two of you chance to meet."

Their conversation is cut off by their food orders arriving.

Rachael, knowing it will be an overcast day tomorrow, puts her water glass down and invitingly announces,

"Lucy, how about tomorrow you and I spend the day together, while Victor takes Benjamin for a ride around Sleepy Hollow on his classic Harley-Davidson Motorcycle. There's a little Lady's shop up on the road we can walk to, also if you'd like to we could stop in at the nearby, Horseman Tavern for a little lunch with a glass of wine, it will be my treat, of course."

"That, Rachael, sounds simply fab!"

"Decent, then it's a happenin', Lucy!"

Rachael sitting in the Riverside Inn lobby just waiting for Lucy to come down from her room, Mike comes into the lobby from the kitchen to see her there, so questions her,

"Rachael, can I help you with anything?"

She explains why she is there to him and then requests of him,

"Mike, I'm going outside into the parking lot. When Lucy comes down please tell her where I am."

"No problem will do."

Rachael steps outside on the deck to see young Ben at Victor's' Harley polishing the front fender to a mirror finish.

He hears behind him, her footsteps on the asphalt and stops to turn round to greet her,

"Hello, Rachael, just cleaning up the Bike a little, while I'm waiting for Victor, to take me for my ride around Sleepy Hollow."

"I know that Victor, being a southern man, will appreciate that very much, Ben."

"I sure hoped he would."

"Oh, he will, he will very much."

Ben softly, replies,

"This Cycle is oh so Bit-chin, and those leather saddlebags on the rear fenders are just so classic. Really so retro, just so extremishly Boss!"

Lucy appears on the deck and excitedly calls to Rachael,

"Hey Rach, I'm all ready to go!"

"Okay Ben have a fun time and please be safe, just do what Victor tells you to."

Then she starts to walk to Lucy announcing,

"Good, we can go out the door on the other side of the Inn."

Ben nicely, but loudly calls out to them both,

"You Ladies have yourselves an awesome day now, catch you later!"

They both appreciatively give him a thumbs-up gesture and enter the Lobby.

Walking, Victor enters the parking lot from the street entrance.

Ben questions him,

"Why yeah coming in from the street?"

"Well my boy, I was just having myself a look-see at the road condition, we need to be aware of any new potholes that can develop overnight, they can be terribly hazardous to anyone when driving a Motorcycle."

"Yup, Victor you're sure right about that."

"So, if you're ready kid? Let's get going now!"

Victor mounts the Bike, fervently Ben gets up behind him and they both put on a Helmet. Victor pushes down the starter peddle and the Bike roars to life, walks the Bike in reverse, turns the front wheel to the street exit, and off they go.

15.

Rachael And Lucy, walk through the Lobby to the side door on the other end of the Riverside Inn. Just as they make their way to Riverside Road, the roaring sound of a Harley Davidson Motorcycle engine attains their attention so they quickly look in the direction of the sound, to observe Ben seated behind Victor, as his Motorcycle quickly proceeds down the road.

They walk along quietly as they approach the street that will take them up to the Main Road, where the A.B. Ladies Shop is located. As they reach the Main Road and begin to walk in the direction of the Shop, Lucy requests,

"Rachael, you are going to tell me how you met Victor, right?"

"Yes, Lucy, when we have our Lunch, let's just do a little shopping first. Okay?"

"Oh Yes, Rach, girl talk over lunch will be just like old times!"

Rachael ruminates,

I will relate to her, just what I told Victor that I would tell her, about our meeting each other and falling in love in Washington DC, not the accurate truth, of course, but one that should satisfy her insatiable curiosity.

They enter the shop, to be greeted by Rose, who recognizes Racheal right off, expressing,

"Why, Miss Rachael it is sure enough good to see y'all back here at the Shop. And I'm ah seeins you've done brought yeah self a friend."

"Yes, Rose this is my childhood friend Lucy from back home, she's here visiting with me and Victor for a little while."

"Well, It's mighty nice to be ah meetins y'all Miss Lucy, needins any hep I'm here fir yeah, sure."

As they walk away into the Shop from Rose, Lucy leans into Rachael and whispers,

"Southern girl up here in Sleepy Hollow. A little strange, huh?"

"Yup, kind of a long and somewhat sad story, I'll tell you about it sometime."

"Okay,"

Lucy immediately finds and picks out something off the rack and says,

"Now, this is real pretty and just my size too!"

Rachael then finds a few things she likes and they go up to the small checkout counter where Rachael pays for it all and they take their leave of the Shop, expressing grateful goodbyes all around.

Now at the Horseman Tavern to have their lunch, they take a small table for two away from the bar.

U.S. Marshal, Special Agent, Michael Aggelos leisurely walks along the streets of downtown Houston Texas, which are noted on the map, made and given to him by Houston Police Officer Angela Garcia, he wears his plain street clothes and a newly purchased Cowboy Hat, just getting the lay of the land in daylight hours. He just happens to notice a small, what looks to be an old rundown unused Basilica, set back from the street, he thinks that this could be a base for what this so-called Mr. Hyde could be using for doing his malicious things to women, so he stops to make a note of it on the map and also he'll file its location in his memory.

After checking out all the alleged assault locations on the map and marking them as such, he begins to walk back to his Hotel, coming across a small sandwich shop he enters to have a quick bite to eat. While he enjoys his sandwich he roughly triangulates the places on the map, to find that in the center of them is that small rundown Basilica, he had discovered set back from the street, thinking,

This old forsaken Basilica will be my first place of interest for this culprit to be based, in my memories of Angel Seraph which I have recently replaced in her mission of helping the people here, there is a similar case that was an old Cathedral in France, that was used in this manner, by something rather evil. This person, just might not be a genuine evil entity, but still, it seems to be acting upon evil intentions that must be stopped straight away, before a defenseless woman is hurt badly or murdered.

Finished now with his meal and his map research he takes his leave of this Sandwich Shop and continues on his way to his Hotel to rest and relax until nightfall approaches when he will do his first stakeout of this place that his investigation has him strongly believing to be this culprit's base of his evil operations.

The order of a glass of red wine and a white wine spritzer are brought by the Bartender to the table of Rachael and Lucy. He then informs them,

"We have a nice, very fresh Roast Beef sandwich today. Might you both be liking one?"

Rachael looks to Lucy as they both agree to have one.

"Yes, Joe, we will have one each, please."

He leaves them to get their order.

Lucy lowers her wine glass to the table and addresses Rachael,

"Okay, now Rach how did you and Victor meet?"

Rachael, takes a moment, to gather her thoughts and begins,

"Okay, so Lucy you remember when I told you in New York City I was going to Washington DC to check on my first book Copyright registration, right?"

"Yup. And?"

"Well, it checked out just fine all was done, but before I was to leave and get back here to Sleepy Hollow, I decided I'd get something to eat before I hit the road. I spotted the Capital Grill Restaurant and decided to go in for lunch, unfortunately for me, it was just a little after noontime, and the place was extremely busy with a wait of about an hour to be seated. Fortuitously, after a few minutes of waiting the Hostess came to me and asked if I'd mind sharing a table with a person eating alone, if so she could seat me right away.

And that person was Victor, and it was like love at first sight, just as my Dad had written in his memoir about my Mom when they first met. He worked close by and had a company-issued Studio Apartment in the City, we spent a few lovely days together, and when he decided to leave his job and come with me to live here, I said yes let's go. He tied up some loose ends at his job and we were off, and you know the rest."

"Wow, Rach, what an awesome story, sounds like a really fetch romance movie!"

"So, Lucy there you have it. And he is a wonderful man and lover!"

Lucy remarks,

"And might I say gorgeous too!"

"Yes, I must agree with that. He is my fine-looking man!"

At that very moment, Joe delivers their sandwiches. They thank him and he returns to behind the Bar.

Lucy puts down her sandwich and has one last one-word inquiry, "Marriage?"

"It is a possibility, yes!"

"Me, your Maid of Honor?"

"Also a possibility, yes!"

"Sweet!"

They both raise their wine glasses in a premature toast and a little laugh, actually more like a girlish giggle. With their lunch now finished Rachael pays their lunch bill at the bar, and they quit the Tavern heading leisurely back to the Inn.

16.

U.S. Marshal Special Agent Michael Aggelos, now outfitted in his U.S. Marshals uniform and wearing on his waist a small, but powerful side arm weapon, feels that it is just about dark enough outside, so he finishes his last cup of coffee, in the Hotel lounge before heading out to the small Basilica building he located earlier in the daylight, to do his initial stakeout for this case in downtown Houston Texas. As he walks in the direction of this small neglected Basilica, he has a powerful angelic feeling that this is the place where his Mr. Hyde character holds up awaiting for his unsuspecting female victims to appear.

If this proves to be the place he believes to be, this Mr. Hydes' haven, and he does attempt to attack a woman, so as not to endanger her, he will just vocally scare him off, proofing that his angelic feelings are ingenuous, and then he will once again have a meeting with Police Officers Burgoa and Garcia to set up the sting, and capture operation with them.

U.S. Marshal Michael benevolently awaits hidden within the darkness on the side of this old building.

Rachael and Lucy, now back at the Inn, sit relaxing in the lobby, just quietly reminiscing a little about their younger days growing up back in Mystic, Connecticut. Suddenly the side door of the lobby opens, and Ben excitedly enters proclaiming,

"Wow! That was the most awesomely awesome thing to be riding around Sleepy Hollow on the back of a totally Bit... I mean a Rad Classic Harley!"

Mike at the check-in counter hearing Ben about to say Bit-chin, lifted his head just as Ben caught himself and changed it to Rad, making Mike smile at him, then right behind Ben, Victor entered smiling and announced to all,

"Yes, Benjamin we did have some fun today."

And then he looks over to address Rachael and Lucy,

"I surely hope you Ladies did also?"

"Yes, Victor we Ladies did have a very nice day, so glad we all had a truly pleasant day, and now I need to go up and get freshened up to be ready for dinner later."

Mike overhears her and announces to all,

"My sister, Chef Jeannie has been busy today preparing a special reunion dinner for you young Ladies!"

Rachael approaches Mike laying her hand on his and says,

"Your sister is the sweetest woman ever."

"Yes and don't forget part owner of this place and a superb cook, to boot!"

Ben chimes in,

"Yup, she's the best Chef here in Sleepy Hollow!"

"That's right Ben, now go in the kitchen and see if she needs your help with any prepping work."

With an ever-so-restrained mutter, Ben quits the lobby for the kitchen.

Rachael asks of Mike,

"So Mike, what is this Special meal Chef Jeannie is cooking up for us?"

Mike just smiles sneakily and answers her,

"Well Rachael, sorry my dear but, she has sworn me to secrecy, and I wouldn't want to spoil the surprise she has for you and your friend Lucy, and whatever you do, please don't ask Ben, I don't think he knows what it is anyway."

"Oh Mike, you people are the best, see you later for dinner."

"Yes, for a Special dinner, tonight!"

U.S. Marshal, Michael Aggellos is waiting patiently deep within the shadows on the side of this old structure, suddenly he catches what sounds like a woman's high-heel shoes coming down the sidewalk, approaching him from his right, he becomes extremely alert, just about holding his breath, listening to the sound of her shoes coming closer to him. When this woman reaches the front of the Basilica she stops to wait and no sooner does a vehicle arrive for her, the passenger door swings open so she enters the automobile, closes the door and it quickly pulls away, and Michael softly exhales. He thinks,

Okay so, no action this time, I kind of have mixed feelings now, I am glad this woman wasn't molested, but I also wish this Mr. Hyde

had shown himself, then I'd know this was the right place for him to use as his base.

He fingers the handle of his weapon in its holster remembering,

My sidearm is only loaded with rubber bullets so I will not be able to kill anyone, which is not acceptable to my non-earth-bound superiors, still, these projectiles are and should be lethal enough to disable just about any person long enough for me to apprehend them, into custody.

Unexpectedly, he hears the squeaking of old rusty door hinges, so he carefully peers around the wall at the front double doors, sort of, in a way, as luck would have it for him, the door closest to him is being opened, which blocks any view for Michael, to see who it could be opening this door, also it's obstructing this person's view of him seeing who could be observing him opening the door. Michael now noticed, by the light of a full moon shining on the front of this Basilica, someone slightly poking out their head looking around slowly, wearing an old-looking man's gray hat, comes into his view. When the person attempts to look in Michaels' direction he quickly ducks back, but still, he does get to catch a quick look at this person's slightly distorted-looking face. So he reflects,

It could just be the way the moonlight was reflecting on his face.

Micheal in the need to stretch his legs, quietly walks out in the dark to the sidewalk looking both ways to observe all is quiet and still, no one seems to be around, turning around to view the front of the Basilica he notices what seems to be a small candle flame flickering at a distance inside, coming from one of the windows which are on each side of the front doors. He decides he'll go back to his hiding place to wait a little longer, but nothing happens, so he calls it a night and heads back to his Hotel, strangely when he quickly looks back the flickering flame light is no longer showing through the window. As he walks along he considers,

There's definitely someone lurking within this building, or even residing in it, I now strongly believe my angelic intuition is right about this disregarded and discounted location, I will return after getting some intel about this place, hopefully, tomorrow at the Houston City Library.

In their room, Rachael and Victor clean up and begin to ready themselves to go down for their special surprise dinners.

Victor in front of the full-length mirror while tying his tie, hears Rachael come out from the Bathroom, speaking softly inquiring,

"So, Rach you did tell Lucy what you told me you would about how we met?"

"Yes, Vic I did after we did a little shopping at the A.B. Ladies Shop, while we had our lunch at the Horseman Tavern, and wait till you see what I bought!"

His eyes widen and turns to her saying,

"Wow, two surprises in one night, first a special dinner, and then you wearing some new, I'd hazard a guess, sexy sleepwear!"

"Well my love, for both, you will need to wait a little, first dinner, and then for me for your dessert!"

Victor smiles and, replies softly,

"Mmmm, they both sound delicious!"

Rachael gives him a wry smile.

At that very moment, their conversation is interrupted by a soft knocking on their room door,

"Hello, Rachael, Victor, it's me, Lucy. Are you two ready to go down for dinner yet?"

Rachael walks over to the door to answer her.

"Lucy we're just getting dressed now, why don't you go down to the lobby and tell them that we'll be down shortly."

"Okay, Rach see you both down there soon."

Rachael turns to Victor and says,

"You may have to wait a little longer for your dessert, after dinner I will need to go down to the river's edge and get a quick Blood fix from an animal."

"Rach, now that you mention it you do look slightly pale."

"Well, I can fix that with a little cover-up makeup for when we have our special dinner."

Lucy goes down to the lobby and is greeted by Mike and Ben.

Mike addresses her from the check-in counter, as Ben quickly stands up from his Lobby bench.

"Good evening, Lucy don't you look very lovely this evening!"

Ben chimes in,

"She looks super fab!"

Lucy blushes, saying,

"Why thank you, boys, it's just a little something new I found at the A.B. Ladies Shop that Rachael bought for me!"

Ben has a thought,

I'll say, it's little, wow!

Lucy announces,

"Rachael and Victor should be down shortly, and my goodness something from the kitchen smells absolutely awesome!"

Ben reacts,

"What you are smelling Lucy is your Special surprise dinner cooking. May I get you anything while you are waiting, anything at all?"

"I could use a cup of coffee, please Ben."

"I do remember how you like it, back in a flash!"

Mike comments to Lucy,

"You do realize, my dear, you now have that boy in the palm of your hand."

"Mike, It wasn't my intention to do so."

"I know, he's just at that age."

Ben returns with the coffee for Lucy and declares,

"Chef Jeannie informed me, that dinner will be served in about twenty minutes."

Rachael and Victor start making their way down the stairs to the lobby. While walking down Rachael remarks,

"Wow! What a wonderfully terrific smell coming from the kitchen, we could smell it, all the way, upstairs in the hallway!"

Ben excitedly informs them all,

"Dinner in twenty minutes!"

17.

U.S. Marshal, Special Agent Michael Aggelos, once again in his street clothes, having his morning meal in his Hotel's breakfast area asks the person seated next to him if they know where the Houston Public Library is, they answer him,

"Sorry, not from around here, just on a short getaway break from my job in Auston, you could ask at the concierge desk they should know."

"Thanks ya'll, I'll be doins' just that as soon as I'm ah finished here with my meal, sorry to be bothering y'all."

"It's no bother Sir, have a nice day."

"Yup, you also my friend."

They both go back to eating.

Michael approached the concierge desk and asked, about the City's Public Library location, he was told its address, which is only two blocks away from the Hotel, and after thanking them for the help, he then left to walk to it. At the Library he finds that this old Basilica is considered to be a historical building constructed on the orders of General Sam Houston in the early eighteen hundreds and that the City had to build around it. He was given a blessing on what was then just a vacant lot of land by the City's residing Cleric, before setting out on his mission to find and capture the Mexican Leader Santa Anna, who ordered the attack on the Alamo, so before General Houston's departure he ordered the construction of it to begin. Michael closed the book of copies of historical documents, sat back, and just said quietly,

"Amazing!"

On leaving the Library he slowly walks a little just enjoying the pleasant Houston weather, thinking,

I'll go back to the Basilica tonight in my street clothes and act like a man coming down the street and regrettably come upon this alleged culprit making his appearance endeavoring to accost an innocent female, that should put him off from doing any real harm to her, and I should get a good look at him, then knowing it is the right place to catch him in the act, then accompanied by the Houston Police Officers, come back to put an end to his reign of terror on the women of Houston.

At the Riverside Inn dining room front table which has a large picture window giving a lovely view of the Hudson River, in the Inn of Sleepy Hollow, New York State, this early evening's guests of honor, Rachael, Victor, and Lucy just patiently enjoying the view and their drink order, Ben comes to the table carrying a silver tray of a water pitcher and the glasses and a basket of fresh still warm rolls and the butter. Placing the tray on the server's folding stand, he provides each of them with a water glass at their setting, then puts the water pitcher in the center of the table, he then looks over to Lucy, she looks up at him, and he swiftly diverts his eyes, from the top of her newly acquired low-cut black dress, to her eyes, she seductively and ever so sweetly inquires of him,

"Benjamin, my sweet handsome boy, do you happen to know…"

Quickly he answers her, with his head turned toward the kitchen nervously declaring,

"Nope, nothing, I know nothing, nothing at all and I saw nothing also!"

Then placing the basket and butter on the table, he grabs the empty tray and quickly goes back to the kitchen.

Rachael gently taps Lucy's hand and says,

"Lucy leave the kid alone."

"Rach I just wanted to…"

"Lucy I know what you wanted, so just be patient and enjoy your wine and have yourself a nice warm roll."

With a slight huff, she takes a sip of her wine.

Chef Jeannie in her chef attire comes from the kitchen over to their table,

"Well, how are all of you this evening? Hungry I hope!"

Lucy answers her,

"Yes, hungry and wondering what it is you have cooked for us!"

"That will be revealed very soon, first your wait person will serve you my very own specialty appetizer I have made for you all."

Rachael once again puts her hand on Lucy's to stop her from saying anything further and comments to Jeannie,

"I am quite sure we will enjoy whatever you have especially created for us."

"Good, it will be out soon, enjoy!"

Chef Jeannie returns to the kitchen.

A moment later their waitperson appears with a tray places it on the folding stand, distributes a small saucer to each of them, and then places a plate of assorted medallions of meat at the center of the table. Simply saying,

"Please enjoy, with compliments of Chef Jeannie!"

They shared and enjoyed the appetizers, slightly for the time delaying their hunger for the special main course.

U.S. Marshal, Special Agent Michael Aggelos, is just killing time until nightfall, leisurely walking the City naturally, as a Tourist would do, modestly taking in the sights and sounds of this historical Metropolis. He decides to go to the Basilica for a more intense look at it in the daylight, and this time he will walk around the building peering into the windows and looking for alternate ways of entry or exit, other than the front wooden double doors hoping to see something of interest inside to help with this strange case.

Finding no more than his earlier observations have given him, he goes back to walking the street. It's now getting near lunchtime and he's beginning to feel a little peckish. About two blocks away from the Basilica, he takes note of a wafting of foods from a good-size food cart, with salivating curiosity he approaches it, to find what is being sold, to his delight, there is a southwestern plethora of assorted foods, from spicy savory to sugary sweet. A lovely young female attendant greets him,

"Good afternoon, Sir. Might I be of help to you?"

"Yes, y'all sure can, young lady," He then points at the items he desires, "I'd be ah liken to make the purchase of one this here and one of those there, and a bottle of that there soda pop, thanks y'all, very much."

She packed the items in a bag for him, and he paid her with a small tip, but before leaving her cart with his bundle he asked her,

"Cuse me, Miss, do yous' happens' to know anything about someone who just might livins' in the old Basilica," He points and continues, "Two blocks down this street, that way?"

"I am sorry, but I do not know anything about that, Sir."

With that answer being no help to him, he thanked her, says goodbye, and then went on his way. To find a nice place, where he could sit and eat his food.

Rachael, Victor, and Lucy watched as Ben slowly pushed a silver trolly to their table, followed by their waitperson with another one, they each stopped on opposite sides of the table, and Ben lifted the silver dome to reveal what was under his tray, a variety of sauteed seasoned vegetables. Then on the other side of their table, their waitperson does the same to reveal a three-pound cooked-to-perfection delicious New York sirloin prime rib roast of beef, surrounded by a garnish of gourmet tomato chutney. Chef Jeannie shows up at the table to finish the presentation and to give the servers instructions to serve the food as the diners request their portion amounts.

18.

While Enjoying Their lovely special dinner, Lucy takes a sip of water and excuses herself from the table for the ladies' room, while she's away, Victor leans over to Rachael to ask,

"How are you planning on getting to go out to the River bank alone?"

"After we are finished with dinner, I will skip the dessert and you and I will have a fake verbal argument out in the Lobby and I will storm out alone. If Lucy then tries to follow me you will stop her by telling her, to just let me be on my own."

"Fake verbal argument about what! Rachael?"

"That doesn't matter just play along. Okay, Victor?"

"Yes, yes of course my love, here she comes."

"So hush now, Victor."

With their delicious meal now just about finished, they are informed a special dessert and coffee will be served soon, in a huff Rachael rises from her chair, throws her napkin down onto the table, and proclaims irately,

"I don't want any dessert!"

She hastily leaves the dining room and goes out to the Lobby which is right now unoccupied, usually Mike and Ben are in the Lobby but right now they are both in the kitchen helping out.

Immediately Victor follows her out there. They are heard by all in a verbal confrontation, but unseen they are just faking it, still to all within earshot it sounds real enough so that Rachael can storm out of the Inn alone. Lucy shows up in the Lobby and catches sight of Rachael going out the door, she begins to go after her when Victor quickly grabs her arm and says,

"Lucy just let her go, when she gets like this sometimes, it's best to let her be alone for now."

Victor reasons,

Oh yes, it is best to leave her to attain her much-needed Blood fix on her own, because anyone with her could end up becoming her

victim, which Lucy knows nothing about, and this needs to definitely stay that way.

Victor still gently holding onto Lucy's arm moves in the direction of the dining room saying,

"Come on Lucy let's have some coffee and dessert, we wouldn't want to be rude to Chef Jeannie."

She gently resists him asking,

"But, Victor what about Rachael?"

Just then Mike comes into the Lobby inquiring,

"Victor something happening with Rachael?"

"Mike, she'll be okay we just had a little disagreement and she stormed out, she'll cool off and be back soon, I'm sure she will."

Rachael hastily makes her way to the Hudson River Bank wooded area to find herself a good-sized deer, as she quietly walks along, she brings out her Vampire intensified powers of sight and smell. At the clearing now, she detects no animals, no animals at all. she thinks,

Strange.

She stops to listen and sniff the air, but still nothing. Suddenly, not too distant from her, a light begins to grow brighter and move closer to her location in the clearing.

She questions out loud,

"Dad, could it be you once again?"

She hears a voice seemingly from nowhere,

"It certainly could be him, I mean me, well my Spirit!"

As the light grows slowly larger and brighter two trees lean together to form an arch, like the time before inside this arch, an oval of golden light shows Michael's brilliant white ethereal image of her departed beloved father, Michael Valli.

Racheal goes down on one knee, lowers her head, and retracts the Vampire powers, she had brought out, then declares,

"Father it is you! I mean your Spirit."

"Yes my daughter it is, I've been granted another visit with you and it must always be, just you and I."

A vehicle slowly driving along the River Road, happens to observe the strange glowing light among the trees of Michaels' ghostly visit, but his image can not be seen.

She questions,

"Just you and me, father?"

"Yes, my dear I'm not allowed to appear to anyone else."

"I do believe I know what you want, it's again about me, wanting to have children with Victor."

"You are correct my dear daughter, you must realize that bringing what you want, which will most likely be of your kind, into the world would not be a good thing to do."

"Father, I have been hearing lately that certain people in the living world wish to decrease the Earth's population, So?"

"So, you believe them, that it's a good thing to do?"

"Well, father if, and I'm only saying if, it were to be a good thing I would be sort of helping."

"Rachael please, by anyone aspiring for people to die, to advance their narcissistic life is never a good thing!"

"Father, at your request I will reconsider having offspring."

"Good, my daughter, I sense the pull of being taken back, my time is up for now, I will try to return to you as soon as they make it possible for me to do so."

"Adieu my father, I do love you!"

Once his image has dissolved, and the bright light is depleted, making it dark again in the woods, she lowers her head, stands, and with her full Vampire powers, she looks intensely into the trees, and sure enough, she detects and ascertains through the trees the body heat of a large deer drinking from the brook, just beyond the clearing. She slowly moves to it and makes the kill to acquire the Blood she needs.

She walks somewhat energized back to the Riverside Inn and enters the Lobby, not surprised to find Victor and Lucy sitting in chairs, with Mike at his Check-in counter.

Lucy rises and quickly goes to her asking,

"Rach, are you okay?"

"Yes, Lucy I'm fine. I was just upset about something Victor said to me while you were in the Ladies' room."

She winks at Victor without Lucy seeing her do it, he smiles back at her. Ben enters the Lobby happy to see that Rachael is now back so he declares,

"Rachael good to see you're back, you missed dessert. Would you like some? There's still some left."

"Thanks, Ben, but just a nice cup of hot tea will do for me right now, please."

"Sure thing, Racheal, no prob, coming right up, have yourself a seat, and I still do remember how you like your tea with some honey."

19.

While Enjoying The refreshing cooler evening air of Houston Texas, U.S. Marshal Michael Aggelos sits alone at an outside table at a nearby Coffee shop enjoying a Cappuccino and listening to the sounds of the City's energies.

His cell phone rings, and he answers it,

"Yes, hey, U.S. Marshal Aggelos here. Go!"

"Howdy, Marshal Aggelos, sorry, Michael, it's Officer James Burgoa."

"Yes, Officer what is it, are y'all checkin up on me?"

"No, Michael, just checking in with you Sir, Officer Angela Garcia and I were lately wondering how our, I mean your, Mr. Hyde case investigation is going. Good, we both hope."

"Well, James, I'm makin headway, slowly but surely. Y'all wouldn't want to arrest the wrong person, now would yeah?"

"No, Michael Sir, that ain't never a good thing!"

"I'm ah getten close, so y'all just be patient a might longer now, okay?"

"Yes, Michael we will."

"I'm ah doins' me some more surveillance tonight,

I'll call you both in when I'm ah sure it's the right person to be apprehenden, just be patient now. Y'all hear?"

"Yup, Michael, I hear that, bye."

Michael hangs up and goes back to relaxing. Just as soon as it gets dark he'll execute his plan for tonight. He has himself a strong feeling tonight will reveal the truth about the so-called Mr. Hyde.

U.S. Marshal, Michael Aggelos sat in the lobby of his Hotel enjoying a takeaway Cappuccino just watching the sun get lower in the sky, dark enough now he walks along the street of the location of the historical Basilica, he has had under surveillance for a while now, as the possible abode of this perpetrator, Mr. Hyde. Drinking his coffee and also wearing a small but powerful concealed weapon on his belt, loaded with rubber bullets. As he slowly passes the building he notices the dim flickering light through the same window as before, and just for an instant he sees a face at that window, he continues on his walk now with heightened awareness. At about twenty-five feet away from the building, he hears a woman's loud yell and then loud footfalls coming toward him. This woman runs right into him and he holds her fast by her arms, for she is very frightened and hysterically shouting through her tears,

"He tried to get me! Oh my Lord, he tried to get me!"

"Please, ma'am try to calm down, yeah safe now. Tell me who it was, tried to get y'all?"

She takes a deep breath and speaks nervously,

"Well, he...he sud...suddenly just came out of the darkness at me, he was a big man, okay, I believe it was a man, adorned in an old man's type hat and a shabby overcoat, the smell of him was awful, like an animal. He grabbed me and I screamed, and instantly pulled myself away from him and blindly just started running down the street, right into you, I am so sorry."

"It's okay ma'am, I am a U.S. Marshal working with Houston Police here, with the intent of procuring this here suspect of these attacks, like he just tried on you tonight. Did he happen to say anythin to ya'll?"

"Say...say anything to me?"

"Yes to yeah, ma'am."

"All I...all I heard from him was like an animal growl, Oh my Lord, he tried to get me! Go get him, Officer...I...I mean Marshel."

"Please ma'am try to stay calm. Did y'all happen to see where he went, when yeah pulled yourself away from him and then ran into me?"

"I am very sorry about that, Marshal, but I just ran without looking back, right into you. And I am ever so sorry."

"Ma'am it's okay, and ya'll are very lucky I was out here tonight because he must have seen me and didn't try to pursue y'all. Yeah best be on your way now. But first I'll be ah needins to get your name, address, and phone number, the Houston Police just might want a statement from y'all."

She takes out a small notepad and pencil from her pocketbook writes down her information, tears it from the pad, and hands it to him.

"Yes, yes Off...I mean Marshal, here.

As he looks at the small page of notepaper, in the full moonlight, he announces

"Thanks ya'll, kindly Melanie, and ya take care now."

She briskly walks off, down the street.

And Marshal Michael walks back to the Basilica with even more heightened awareness, if it's, at all possible. The first thing he observes is that the dim flickering light in the window he saw earlier, is now out. He just stands looking at the building deliberating in his mind,

I know you're in there and we're going to get you, very soon.

In the mid-afternoon of the day after the special dinner at the Riverside Bed and Breakfast Inn, in Sleepy Hollow New York State, the local Police Captain Nickels, intensely calls his on-duty desk Sargent into his office.

"Yes Sir. What do you need, Sir?"

"Well, Sargent this report from last night just came across my desk, about a driver seeing a strange bright light in the woods along the Hudson River bank, right near the area of the Riverside Bed and Breakfast Inn, and I want it checked out immediately, like right now, today! Call the car on patrol in that district and give them the information from this report," he hands the report across his desk to the sergeant and continues, "and tell them I want their findings report by the end of today's shift."

"Yes Sir, will do pronto!"

The patrolling Police Officers receive Captain Nickels's orders and they arrive at the appointed location, at first they find nothing unusual, still on closer observation one of them notices the strange wrinkling of the tree bark on the two adjacent trees that seems to have leaned into each other and then back up straight in their natural state. The other Officer checks around near the river's edge and sees a large Deer's carcass floating along the shoreline. He calls to his partner,

"Jeff, come have a look at this!"

Jeff sees the body and responds,

"Yeah so, a dead Deer, we've seen these before. So what's the big deal, Johnny?"

"It just looks kind of flat to me. Doesn't it to you?"

"Okay yeah kind of, so grab it by the antlers and pull it ashore. And we'll get a closer look at it."

Officer John drags it up on the dry bank and they see nothing unusual, so they flip it over, and then they both notice something weird. Two puncture wounds on its neck.

They look at each other with a puzzled expression, they both question,

"Snake bite?"

Jeff responds,

"Much too big a bite for that, I'd say more like, human."

"You think someone tried to eat a live Deer?"

"Not its flesh, maybe just its blood!"

"It's Blood! What kind of human would do that?"

"A human Vampire would!"

"What!… What are you sayin…you think a…okay, we had better call this in right now, and not wait to make out a report!"

They call the station to speak to the Captain for further instructions. After telling him what they found, and what they think, the Captain addresses them,

"Get that Deer's body into your trunk and bring it to the Station's lab right now!"

They do as they are ordered.

The Deer's body is brought into the Lab and placed on an examination table covered with a sheet, but their Forensic Medical Officer is off on location in Terrytown today, so the exam will need to wait until tomorrow.

Back now in his office, the Captain sits at his desk takes a deep breath, and thinks,

We just might need some special help with this…weirdness.

20.

Sleepy Hollows' Police Captain Nickels, after reading it, puts down the forensic report of the Deer found on the river's edge yesterday, he then calls out loudly to the Desk Sargent,

"Sargent Mainerd, come in my office for a minute, please."

The Sargent responds quickly to the Captain's request,

"Yes, Sir you need something, Sir?"

"Yes, I do, go down to the forensic lab and tell forensic Officer Fred Clark, I'd like to speak with him before he leaves for the day."

"Yes, Sir right away."

The Officer carries out the Captain's request,

and comes right back to the Captain's office,

"Captain Sir he says he'll be with you as soon as he clears up the Lab."

"Good, thanks, Sargent."

The Captain leans back in his desk chair and thinks,

If my memory serves me right, I seem to remember there was a female U.S. Marshal, Special Agent in the area, that one of my Motorcycle Patrol Officers had casual contact with her up on Bear Mountain road, not too long ago, and we just might need her back, because this forensic report insinuates that we just might have something rather strange, going on in our quaint little town of Sleepy Hollow.

Forensic Officer Clark shows up at the front desk to proclaim,

"Sargent, I believe the Captain wants to see me."

"Yes he does, just a minute Fred, I'll see if he can see you right now."

The Sargent returns to the front desk,

"Go right in, Fred."

Forensic Officer Clark enters the Captain's office.

"Please, Fred have a seat, wanting to see you about this report about the dead Deer my men found."

"Yup that's what I figured you wanted, so you have questions?"

"I certainly do! What's in your report is rather unbelievable."

"Well, Sir my findings are all based on my medical exam, not any personal opinions."

"Well if that is the truth, and you say here," he points to the report, "that this Deer is lacking just about all its Blood in its body, and you feel another animal did not do this act, what I have a problem with is, you think and believe a human did this."

"The Bite is more Human-sized so...."

"So are you saying that a human type of Vampire did it?"

"It's my best medical conclusion, the saliva sample, shows human, but slightly altered in some way almost like, and this is hard for even me to believe, Sir, it's also from an animal!"

"What...wait, from what animal, Fred?"

"That, Sir. with my equipment I can't determine, sorry."

"Well, then I now believe I know whom I need to see and speak with, maybe, just maybe he can help us with the mystery."

"May I ask who you're speaking of, Sir?"

"Yup you can, Mr. Michael Van Garrett, part-owner with his sister Jeannie who is the Chef, and may I say, a real great one, and he as the full-time manager of the Riverside Bed and Breakfast, this act did take place nearby there, perhaps maybe, it just could be, he saw or knows something that could shed some light on this mysterious event."

"And if he can't, I believe we will need some other help, some special help."

"Special help, Sir?"

"Yup, U.S. Marshal, Special Agent type of help!"

"I take it you know who to call at the U.S. Marshal's Department in Washington DC."

"Well, Fred you should know their main contact phone number is known to all law enforcement agencies."

"Yup okay, Sir., good luck, I'll leave you to your investigation."

With that Forensic Officer Clark rises from this chair and quits the Captain's office.

U.S. Marshal, Micheal Aggelos at his Hotel, finishes his morning meal of his favorite Breakfast cereal of Cornflakes with an ample amount of sugar added. He sits back drinking his coffee to make contact with Houston Police Officer James Burgoa to inform him of the event of last night at the Basilica.

Officer Burgoa is very much impressed and agrees, for him and his partner Officer Garcia to meet him this evening at his Hotel, and they will attempt to, no they will, apprehend this Mr. Hyde at the old Basilica.

U.S. Marshal Aggelos reminds him to bring an unmarked vehicle and have Officer Garcia wear her street clothing, she should make it a rather sexy come-on-look appearance, to tempt the perpetrator to attack her while she is lingering on the sidewalk right in front of the Basilica. Officer Burgoa enthusiastically proclaims,

"Michael, tonight we shall get this Mr. Hyde maniac!"

"Yeah, James, you and Angela will, while I'll be your backup, while you two will finally put an end to his Reign of Terror on these here womens' of Houston, Texas."

Michael Aggelos takes the rest of the day to have a leisurely walk around the City in the area surrounding the old historical Basilica, he stops in front of it and lingers for a while just thinking how and why it had come to be built, those many years ago, and what it is being used for now by this, what has to be, a very disturbed individual, that definitely needs to be stopped and hospitalized, or probably institutionalized.

He then reasons,

All the credit for this abduction will go to the two Houston Police Officers who were tasked with this zany case, to begin with, but had so many other duties to perform that they couldn't give their undivided attention to it, which is why I was called in to help out. Still, they started the case and they will get all the credit for finishing it. The credit for my involvement in it will come from Director Hughes of the U.S. Marshal's Department in Washington DC.

Now coming out of his in-depth thoughts, continuing his walk, right on cue, his cell phone rings and the caller ID shows Director Hughes's Office. He answers it,

"Hello, Agent Aggelos here."

"Yes, Agent I have a call for you from the Director, Please hold."

"A course."

A moment passes.

"Hello, Agent Michael, sorry to be bothering yeah, I just needed to contact you about the case you are on in Houston, Texas, and about something going on in the upper State of New York you may be needed for soon."

"Well, Sir., this here case in Houston is ah goins' okay, should be all wrapped up this here very night."

"Good, just keep me posted, and also if and when we can just fly you and your Harley to New York when it's all over down there. Okay?"

"Sure will do that, Sir."

"Okay good, bye."

"Adios, Director Sir."

As he was talking on the phone with the Director while continuing with his leisurely walk through the streets of Houston, Texas, he stopped in front of the City's Library thinking of going in, but he changed his mind and headed back to his Hotel. It only being early afternoon he will relax for tonight's event at the Basilica, for he will need his full faculties about him for sure. It is beginning to become dark, so Michael is relaxing in the Hotel Lobby while having a cup of Coffee and a quick snack, his cell phone sounds off,

"Hello?"

"Hello, Michael, Officer Angela and I are in the parking lot in an unmarked car, a Black Dodge Charger. Are you ready to go?"

"Oh yeah, very much ready for the takedown of this Mr. Hyde! Be with yous' two, in just a mere moment."

The unmarked car is now parked about two blocks away from the Basilica and Michael and James get out to quietly make their way to a hidden place on the dark side of the building, while Angela hangs back to slowly walk alone down the sidewalk. Micheal moves to the only window on this side of the building, and quickly he looks in to see the dim flickering flame of a single candle on a small pedestal lit up. He smiles wryly when he then notices a shadow crossing the room headed to the front doors of the building.

He steltfully makes his way back to James and whispers,

"He's sure enough's in there, James, I saw his shadow on the opposite wall moving toward them there front doors."

"Angela is out front right now Michael, with her back toward the Basilica, making it like she's trying to find something in her purse, by the light of the street lamp."

In their hiding place, they both hear the soft creaking sound of the front doors opening. Micheal takes a firm hold of Jameses' arm, just in case he wants to make a move to help out. Michael reminds him,

"We move in only after she takes him down and has him in the handcuffs that are in her purse."

"Yup, okay, you can let me go now."

Michael releases James' arm as they watch Mr. Hyde quietly coming up behind Angela, she acts like she's unaware of him approaching her, playing her part of the innocent female enticement. He quickly wraps his arms around her and grunts.

Standing about even with him she throws her head back to give him a headbutt, he stumbles back releasing her, and she moves forward and turns to face him with a spinning kick to the side of his head, causing him to stagger a little, but he stays upright, James seeing this begins to make a move, but Michael holds him fast and sharply implies,

"No! James, let her finish him off!"

James relaxes in full agreement with Michael.

She then quickly spins again using her other foot, landing another more forceful blow to the other side of his head, which whirls him around and he goes down hard to the sidewalk on his stomach, quickly takes out the handcuffs from her purse she forcibly moves his arms onto his back and, planting her knee insistently on his back, and applies the cuffs to his wrists. As the men come from their hiding place, with James calling in for the Houston Police Wagon to take him away into custody, Angela stands with one foot on his back, hardly breathing heavily, and triumphantly announces,

"Your Reign of Terror is finished now, monster!"

As the Police Wagon pulls away with this so-called Mr. Hyde person now and finally in custody, they stand smiling at one another under the street lamp, Officer James Burgoa breaks the silence,

"Well, we couldn't have done it without your help, Marshal."

"Nonsense, y'all both would've done it, just woulda' takeins' ya'll a little more time, is all."

21.

Sleepy Hollow Police Captain John Nickels speaks on the phone with Director Hughes of the U.S. Marshals Department in Washington DC, Hughes tells him he would send a Special Agent to Sleepy Hollow as soon as he could because. He explains,

"He needed to finish up helping out the Houston Police on a slightly weird case down there in Texas."

The Captain replies with a confounding question,

"He?... I was not too long ago informed by one of my Motorcycle Officers, that your Special Agent is a Woman, he had had a friendly run-in with her a while back up on Bear Mountain Road along our Hudson River Bank. So he... wait!...um, oh never mind, just send us whom you can, please."

"It has been arranged, so be patient. Our Special Agent Michael Aggelos will be with you soon. Okay?"

"Looking forward to meeting with...him, and having the help, Sir., thanks."

The Captain hangs up his desk phone, leans back in his chair to take a moment to contemplate,

Is it just me, or are things starting to get a little strange around here? Good Lord, what's next, a for-real Headless Horseman shows up, riding around Sleepy Hollow cutting off heads. I believe I need a drink.

At that very moment his Smartwatch chimes that it's noon, he says softly out loud,

"Good, it's lunchtime," Rising from his desk chair he continues in thought,

I'll go up to the Horseman Tavern for a bite to eat and maybe a shot of some of their good Scottish Whiskey.

On his way out, he informs the Desk Sergeant that he's going out to lunch, and quits the station.

After having lunch, without the Whisky, the Captain stops by the Riverside Bed and Breakfast Inn, to speak with the part Owner and Manager Mr. Michael Van Garrit. He enters the Lobby from the deck at the side door where the parking lot is located, Mike hears the door chime sound so he lifts his head from his paperwork to surprisingly see, the Police Captain enter, so he addresses him cordially,

"Good afternoon Captain Nickels. What can I do for you, Sir?"

"Well, Mr. Van Garrit, I'm not sure but, right near here on the River bank we've had some strange goings on, just wondering if you know anything about that might help me get to the bottom of this weirdness."

"Like what kind of strange things happening Captain? And please just address me as, Mike."

"Okay, Mike, And you please call me John, well, my investigation is just getting started."

At the beginning point in their conversation, Racheal started to quietly descend the stairs to the Lobby, when she overheard them talking, she instantly stopped on the second step of the staircase where they could not see her just to listen to what was being said.

"So you can't say much about it. I'd gather."

"Yup, something like that, Mike."

"John, is there anything you can say, that I could help you with somehow?"

"Well Mike what I can say is, a report came in, about a motorist driving north on Riverside Road happening to notice a bright light in the woods along the river bank the other night, and the next day I had two of my Officers sent in to investigate, and the only thing they found was a dead Deer floating in the water at the edge of the river, and at their first look it was not slain by any conventional weapons they know of, the really strange thing is there was no Blood found at the scene in the water or on the ground anywhere, and even more baffling, the cause of death according to our Forensic Officer Clark is a major loss of Blood."

"And you, Captain, suppose I would know anything about this?"

"Well Mike, I just need to follow up on anything I can think of that might help, and speaking of help, I've called and asked the U.S. Marshals' to send a Special Agent to help us with this."

Now seated on the top step, Rachael hears this and thinks,

Well, it won't be Special Agent Angel Seraph coming, that's for sure.

"Okay, John sorry I couldn't be of any help to you, at this time, but if I see or hear anything strange or weird, I'll be sure to contact you."

The Captain turns to head for the door, as he's heading out he says,

"Thanks, Mike, bye, you have a good rest of your day."

"You also John. Bye."

Rachael slowly rises, and quietly heads back to her room to inform Victor about what she has heard in the Lobby. Before she enters the room, to discover that Victor is playing around with her father's Janus medallion by flipping it like it's a coin. When she does open the door abruptly, it startles him and he drops the medallion on the floor.

U.S. Marshal Special Agent Michael Aggelos has now returned to his residence in Baton Rouge, Louisiana from Houston, Texas. In what was once Angels' Condo, which is now his Earthly place of residing, he goes first to the refrigerator to get himself a cold bottle of beer, he sits on the couch to enjoy it and relaxes, reflecting,

Mmm, so good, nothing like this, where I come from. So it's back to Sleepy Hollow, first a good night's sleep, here in my now earthly dwelling. Then come morning, I'll call for the U.S. Marshals' Jet plane to fly me and my Harley to New York City, and then a lovely scenic Motorcycle ride up north to Sleepy Hollow. Hopefully, I can get a room again at the Ichabod Crain Inn, it was rather nice there, should maybe call them first before I call the pilot for the flight.

In the morning after a satisfying restful night's sleep and having his breakfast of his favorite cereal, he made both calls to make the arrangements for a room in the place up there in the lovely little Town of Sleepy Hollow, where he liked to stay at and then called the U.S. Marshal pilot for the flight to New York City.

After his second cup of coffee, he hastily packs his rucksack with the clothing he thinks he will be needing, then gathers and places his firearms, which are already loaded with rubber bullets, with what he supposes he will be needing into his weapons case for this assignment, up there in Sleepy Hollow, and then heads out to the Baton Rouge, Louisiana Metropolitan Airport, once cleared by customs he just hangs out to wait for the Plane to land on the Tarmac, where his Harley will be loaded into the cargo hold and for him to board.

22.

U.S. Marshal, Special Agent Michael Aggelos drives his Harley down the ramp out of the Cardo Hold with his Rucksack and Weapons Case safely in the two saddlebags on each side of the back wheel, then heads to Sleepy Hollow to check into his room at the Ichabod Crain Inn. After settling into the room he makes a call to Director Hughes' office of the U.S. Marshals Department in Washington DC.

"Hello, Director Hughes' office. How can we help you?"

"Yes hello, this here is Special Agent Michael Aggelos, lookins' to be ah speakins' with Director Hughes, please."

"Please hold!"

He's on hold for a moment.

The Director suddenly answers the call,

"Hello, Michael! How was your trip?"

"Mine trip was just fine, Sir."

"Good to hear that, I have spoken with the Sleepy Hollow Police Captain John Nickels, he is expecting you. Would tomorrow at his office be good for you? If so I'll call him and inform him you'll be in at about one pm. That be alright for you?"

"That, Sir sounds just fine with me, and I do knows where their Police station is ah beins'."

"Okay good, Michael, he'll fill you in on what they know and introduce you to the Officers who found the strange item causing their enigma of an incident of interest to them. And Michael, I've received your report from the Houston case, weird case indeed, still having the local Police handle the capture was a very decent thing for you to do."

"Well Sir, they did do what they could, on top of handlins' their day-to-day Policins' duties, they were just ah needins for someone who could focus on their suspect's movements and find out their base of operation, to be ah makin it sure so they could get 'em, that there correct perpetrator into custody."

"Good work down there, now see what you can do to help them out, up there in Sleepy Hollow."

"That's ah pretty much, what I am's ah fixin on doin fir 'em, Sir."
"Okay Michael, good luck, talk soon! Bye."
"Thanks yah Sir, bye, fir now."

With the call ended, he headed out for a leisurely evening stroll to the nearby Horseman Tavern for an early supper.

In their second-floor room of the Riverside Bed & Breakfast Inn. Rachael severely proclaims to Victor,

"Stop playing with my father's Janus medallion, and sit down we need to talk!"

"Why, Rach, what's so urgent?"

"I will tell you, just put the medallion down and listen to me, please."

He sits at the desk, puts the Medallion down, and replies,

"Okay, alright, tell me what is so important, as we say down south, before you bust a gut!"

"Yup, bust a gut! Victor this is serious, we could be in really big trouble, please just listen to me!"

She begins by telling him all that she overheard while sitting on the top step where she could not be seen by anyone down in the Lobby, but knew who they were by them mentioning each others' names while they were having their discussion, which she is now so concerned with.

Victor comments,

"So, the Police found a dead Deer on the Hudson River bank. What about it? I'm sure they are found, all the time, around here. I'm more concerned about someone driving by and seeing a bright light in the wooded Riverbank, just about the time you were out there."

"Yup, a bright light, I'll get to that in a minute, first let me explain about the problem with the dead Deer they found."

"A problem with the dead Deer they found, what problem?"

"Victor sweetheart, Please, I'm trying to tell you about that."

He stands and says irately,

"So okay tell me!"

She begins to explain, speaking rather hurriedly,

"Okay the problem with the Deer was that after I spoke with my father's spirit in the Riverbank woods and then killed the Deer I was in a rush to get back here so I neglected to dispose of the carcass the correct way which is pitching it way out into the river, so I just slid it into the water hoping the current would take it away, but it didn't, that's why they found it, and had it examined to find, my bite mark on its neck and the absence of any Blood in its body."

"Wait, hold on a second, did you just say you spoke with your late father's spirit in the Riverbank woods?"

"Yes, why are you so surprised? I told you I had spoken with his spirit before in the Riverbank woods."

"No, you did not! This is the first time I've heard or you've mentioned to me about that happening here, in Sleepy Hollow."

"I'm very sorry Victor, I really thought that I had told you he had appeared to me before the night in question."

Victor retorts with a bit of anger, but really more like disappointment in his voice,

"Well, no you didn't, and I really can't imagine why you wouldn't have!"

"If I didn't, it's, well because I just thought you'd think I was losing my mind, sorry I should have told you right away."

"Yes, you should have, but let us for now just focus on what to do about and say to this Police Captain Nickels and this new Special U.S. Marshal Agent person who is coming or is most likely already here in Sleepy Hollow."

"Off the top of my head, Victor I'd have to say we just play dumb."

"Okay, we'll go with that, unless we can think of something better before we get questioned by either of them or both."

"Okay Victor, will do."

Victor stops pacing the floor and sits down on the bed.

"Now, Rachael, tell me more about you speaking with your late father's spirit down on the Riverbank."

She sits in the desk chair and begins,

"He appears to me, and he says only to me, and just when I'm alone, within a bright golden oval of light, and inside that oval, he is an ethereal image with very few human features, just a faint outline of what was his living body, I had seen him this way the very first time I had ever had any contact with him, I mean contact with his spirit form, in the past at the Mystic Cliff House when I lived there in Mystic with my mom," so with sadness in her eyes and her voice, she continues, "and remembering it now, it was a very very, mixed emotions encounter with a father I had never known when he was alive."

Victor understandably responds,

"Oh my dear darling Rachael, I can only try to imagine how you must've felt."

She slowly stands with her eyes starting to well up, so he rises and rushes over to her, to deliver physically his love and Understanding, with a heartwarming affectionate hug.

23.

U.S. Marshal, Special Agent, Michael Aggelos, now seated on the visitor's side of Sleepy Hollow Police Captain Nickel's desk waiting for him to finish his phone call. The Captain hangs up and continues with the report information he started to give to Agent Aggelos,

"Well, Marshal that is just about all we know right now. And let me just say again, Sir we are glad to have you here to help us."

"Captin, I am happy to be here to hep y'all out in any way possible, but yah failed to elaborate on that there bright light that was spotted in the wooded area along yourn River, by the driver of the vehicle just ridin by."

The Captain lowers his head, puts his hand on his forehead, and takes a moment before he replies softly, saying,

"Well, Sir. we really don't have much to go on that, as of right now, and we don't want to speculate on it."

"I does understand that, still, has this here strange lights have been ah seen out there since the night in question?"

"No, no reports of it being seen out there ever since that night, still my guess is it was a person hunting at night, which is against the law around here."

"Yup, just bout everywhere, I'd be ah sayin, and Captin please, cut them dang formalities, just address me as Micheal."

"As you wish, and please do just call me John."

"Okay then John, can I ah be ah seeings this here dead Deer tomorra?"

"Yes, see you in the morning, it would be best then, Michael."

"Yup, John after my breakfast I'll be ah here, fir sure."

"Okay, good, till then have a good night, Michael!"

"You too John, bye."

Agent Aggelos quits the Police Station to have himself a ride along the Hudson River, just to get familiar with where the mile marker is located, in doing this he notices that the Riverside Bed and Breakfast Inn is nearby just about where the Bright Light was spotted in the Riverbank Woods, as the Captain had informed him, it was foreseen.

While Victor and Rachael are waiting for their breakfast orders. Victor leans over to quietly confront her with a question about Lucy,

"Rach, when will Lucy be leaving, to get herself back to New York City?"

"I believe she said, she has her room until the middle of next week. Why do you ask?"

"That means this coming Wednesday. Right?"

"Yes, Victor, I will be driving her to the Train Station in the afternoon. Is there a problem for you, with her staying here?"

"Well, my love, I will be requiring a full Blood Passion feeding within the next few days, maybe you two could go…"

Victor is cut off by Lucy coming to the table and having a seat,

as she takes the chair on the opposite side of the table from them, she proclaims,

"I'm in the mood for something sweet like a Waffle with lots of maple syrup, this lovely morning."

"Lucy, that sounds real awesome, they do make really good ones here, I've had them with the syrup and the powdered sugar, too."

"Rach, that is exactly what I will order!"

"Good, knowing how much you like a very sweet morning meal, you will very much enjoy their Waffle, for your breakfast. And Lucy you did want to be at the Train Station in the afternoon on this coming Wednesday. Right?"

"Yup, and I'm really sad about leaving, It's so lovely here in the town of Sleepy Hollow, and seeing you and spending time together like when we were younger is wonderful. Oh yes, and meeting you, Victor is nice too."

Victor just smiles at her and then turns to Rachael with an anxious look on his face.

"So Lucy why don't you and I go out early tomorrow night, say for a little shopping at the A.B. Ladies' Shop and then my treat at a very nice French restaurant down on the River road, I've been there before and it's really awesome, I just know you will just love it! So what do yeah say to that, girlfriend?"

"What do I say! Rach, I say it sounds Rad, I'm in!

Rachael, with a knowing look, looks to Victor, and he just gives her a satisfying smile, and she just smiles back at him.

The waitperson comes over to get Lucy's order, while Victor just asks for more Coffee. Young Benjamin hears his request and shows up right on cue, to do topups, then places a cup in front of Lucy, and pours her a cup. She looks up at him, as he averts his eyes from looking down at her…,

"Thank you, handsome young man, that's so nice and thoughtful of you."

Ben just claims, "Just my job ma'am," and walks away.

Lucy looks at Rachael with a disappointed smile, then she declares questioningly,

"Ma'am?"

Rachael just wistfully smiles at her, while Victor quickly covers his mouth to hold back a laugh.

Lucy excuses herself to use the Ladies' restroom.

Rachael very quietly leads over to Victor and says,

"You really mustn't use the clearing on the Riverbank tomorrow night, they just may have it under constant surveillance, right now. Go out this afternoon and check down River for a clearing, just stay away from the one we both have been using."

"Yes, Rachael you're definitely right about that, my love.

And Rach, what is it the spirit of your father has made contact with you about, or is that something you can't tell me?"

Rachael observes Lucy heading back to their table and sees her stop to speak to their waitperson just to request extra maple syrup for her waffle. She softly tells Victor they will talk about what it is, that the spirit of her father wants with her, later. They both go silent, as Lucy takes her seat at the table.

U.S. Marshal, Agent Michael Aggelos examines the Deer's body and agrees with their basic early report, but realizes there is a somewhat supernatural element involved, he needs to come up with a plausible answer to this Macabre Mystery, so as, not to start a panic in their lovely town, and also convince them to let him handle the investigation totally on his own.

24.

U.S. Marshal Special Agent, Michael Aggelos, and Police Captain John Nickels await in his office at the Sleepy Hollow Police Station, for the two Officers who had started the investigation of this case, to finish their shift and then come to the Captain's Office.

With the two Officers now arrived, Agent Aggelos, after completing his solitary, intensive investigation, earlier in the day on the Riverbank in the area in question, will now explain his findings and conclusions to all who have been involved with this rather strange case.

Rachael and Lucy leave the A.B. Lady's shop with their purchases and get back to Rachael's car to head to the French restaurant up on Riverside Road.

Victor after having a shower, and dressing rather casually to frequent, later this evening, the Horseman Tavern to find what he requires.

Marshal Aggelos, with the two Officers and the Captain now seated in the Office, begins to explain to all involved in attendance, what he considers from his professional findings, just what had taken place that very night;

"Well, I'll start by sayin that, it ain't all that strange when yeah looks at the evidence with logic and a trained eye in these here kind of thins'. I've seen far too many of 'em, so here is what I surmise; this here incident dids surely take place in that there woods on the Riverbank, and it do seems likely to me that your Captins' thinkins bout some one-night hunting, from what I found is a high possibility. I will explain to y'all in more detail: that dead Deer that you two Officers found floating in the water was taking its last drink of water afor goins to sleep for the night when suddenly the light from the hunter's torch light, that there driver dids see from the road that night, startled it and in the darkness also it ah beins somewhat disoriented, jumped in the direction of the River in its panic drownd and the body washed up on the shoreline, and I notice some of them there blood-sucking Leeches in the water where the two Officers pulled the body onto the shore, and made the water in its lungs drain out. So, no Blood found anywhere just means to me that them Leeches had emselves a big meal that night. Them there Bloodsuckers is also what made the marks on its neck to begin the feast. The human DNA that was detected was most likely from a Leech that had lately sucked on human Blood and picked it up from that there person. So that there is my official report."

The Captain stands and declares with well-acted relief,

"Okay, men this case is officially closed!"

The offices leave, and the Captain sits back down, looks to Marshal Aggelos, and says,

"So that will be the official report for the public. Now please, tell me the truth to it all, Marshal."

"That Captin, I'm ah sure ya'll just might be ah findins' that be a little troublesome to be ah believings'."

"Marshal, I need the truth for myself, I think I can handle it, Sir."

Victor before going to the Tavern, had earlier in the evening found a clearing on the wooded Hudson Riverbank downriver from the one that had been being used by him and Rachael.

Now seated at the bar of the Horseman Tavern, he scans the room for a potential unwilling victim of his much-needed Blood Passion feeding. To his pleasant dismay, he spots what seems to be a younger man than him, glancing in his direction, from time to time, he catches him looking his way, so he smiles at him, and the younger man smiles holding his gaze on Victor.

Victor lifts his wine glass and also points with his empty hand to the unoccupied seat beside him as a juster for him to sit there. The man raises an eyebrow in agreement and moves to the empty seat at the bar next to Victor.

Rachael and Lucy walk to the car in the restaurant parking lot after having a delicious French meal together. As Rachael drives back to the Riverside Bed and Breakfast, Lucy continually keeps thanking Rachael for paying for her meal.

Rachael obstinately replies,

"Lucy please stop, we are childhood friends it was totally my pleasure, to treat you to a nice dinner before you went back to your digs in New York City!"

"Nice! It was fab and I'll bet expansive too!"

Rachael giggles a bit saying,

"No prob girl, you let me worry about that."

"Are you worried?"

"Not at all, just a figure of speech."

"Ok, good I wouldn't want to make you worry about anything."

"I know you wouldn't want that of me. So remind me what time is your train on Tuesday leaving for New York City?"

"Not Tuesday. Rachael, Wednesday, at noon. You trying to get me gone a day earlier, or what?"

"No no, not at all, Lucy just a mind slip! Sorry."

"Like a senior moment, Rach?"

With that said, they both break out into robust laughter.

In Captain Nickel's Office, he asks Marshal Michael Aggelos for the truth realizing the report he just related was not the real report. Marshal Michael Aggelos with his head down, hesitates in thought for a moment, then looks up at the Captain and asks him,

"Captin I ah sure you've read and heard of stories of humans that suck Blood to live. Right?"

"Yup, you mean like Dracula and such? There was that strange fictional story bout a Headless Horseman here in our town that some believed was for real."

"Yes, I do knows bout that one and it made this here town of yourn famous."

"Marshal, please what is it you are getting at?"

"Well, Captin what I'm ah gettins' at is, I truly believes' y'all has is at least one person going around sucking Blood from living beings."

The Captain suddenly stands behind his desk and, softly replies,

"Are you actually saying we have a for real Human Vampire residing here in my town?"

"What I'm ah sayins' is, all the real evidence leads to just that, I'll stays' around this here parts a bit longer to question the locals and the visitors iffin' y'all don't have any objection, that is."

"No, no not any objections, you stay just as long as you feel the need to, Marshal. But what about that bright light that was reported?"

"Okay, Captin that's another reason for me to stays around here, I'ds be ah sayins, so I'll calls my Director to gives him an update in the mornin'."

They wish each other a good night and they both leave the Police station and then go their separate ways.

25.

Rachael And Lucy still softly laughing, return to the Riverside Bed and Breakfast, park in the lot, take their shopping bags out from the back seat of the car, and walk up the three steps onto the deck with the side Lobby entrance, speaking softly to each other they enter, the door chimes sounds, so Mike looks up from his counter paperwork and Ben stands up from his Lobby bench to see who has come in. Mike greets them both,

"Good evening Ladies. Have yourselves a nice time today?"

Racheal answers him,

"Yes, we did and Mike that French restaurant you told us about where my cousin has been to, was totally fab! And we both would like to thank you for suggesting to me that we should go there."

Lucy chimes in,

"Oh yes, it made it an extremely Fetch way to end our day!"

Mike suggests,

"Why don't you two have yourselves a little rest, so please, you both have a sit down in the Lobby. And I am sure," he looks to Ben and continues, "Ben would just love to bring you two a nice hot cup of decaf coffee from our kitchen that is still open for another thirty minutes."

Without a word, they both lollup into an easy chair in the Lobby as Ben quickly proceeds to the kitchen for the Coffee and the fixings.

Ben returns promptly with the Coffees. They thank him, and both enjoy the coffee and then decide to go up to their rooms for a little more rest from their fairly active day out together, also to put away the things they had purchased at the A.B. Ladies Shop, earlier to start their fun girl's night out. In the Lobby, good night wishes are exchanged by all present. On the second floor in the fairly wide hallway at their individual room doors down the way from each other, Rachael softly wishes Lucy sweet dreams, she returns the sentiment, and they both enter their respective rooms. Rachael is presently surprised to find Victor seated cavalierly in the desk chair looking rather full of himself, grinning like; 'The Cat that had Swallowed the Canary'. Rachael inquires,

"So you found what you needed at the Tavern, I take it from the way you look, and you are looking rather good to me."

"And I feel good also after meeting this young man Dave and we…

"Stop right there! No one knows better than me what you did with him."

"Okay now, I want to show you the new lingerie I bought today, so get comfy and I'll be right out to have some special fun together!"

She takes one of the shopping bags and goes into the bathroom proclaiming cutely,

"Be right out, lover, so don't you start without me!"

The next morning Rachael, Lucy, and Victor are at breakfast, Lucy sadly affirms,

"So tomorrow I get my train back to New York City. I will miss this lovely place, you both, and everyone who works and runs this awesome Inn."

"Yes, Lucy we will miss you too. I would guess, Benjamin most of all of the people that work here, will miss seeing your…."

Victor cuts her off,

"Rach, please stop right there!"

Lucy laughs and says,

"He's a handsome young boy, and I'm sure he will be a real hunk of a man someday soon!"

Victor asks Lucy,

"So what will you do on your last full day here?"

"I will certainly take a walk around the neighborhood and get some pictures after breakfast, and speaking of breakfast, I will miss the food here it is oh so fetch!"

Victor extends her an invitation,

"Maybe if you'd like, later this afternoon I could take you on a ride on my Harley around the Hamlet. What do you say to that, Lucy?"

"What do I say! That would be so," she lowers her voice and continues, "Bit-chin for sure!"

Rachael lets out a subdued giggle, while Victor and Lucy just smile. Then they all go back to finishing their morning meals.

U.S. Marshal, Special Agent, Michael Aggelos, looking like a tourist in plain clothes, with his badge wallet in his back pocket and a small concealed rubber bullet loaded handgun, casually walks the streets and roads of the Sleepy Hollow Hamlet, around where the incident he was called on, took place. Being friendly to all he meets, just asking simply if they have seen any strange things in the last few days.

Not making much progress that way, he decides to stop in at the Riverside Bed and Breakfast Inn, which is right near to the location where it all took place the night in question, along the Hudson River, to optimistically find out something from anyone working there or staying there.

The door chime sounds as he enters the Lobby, Ben stands up from the Lobby bench, and looking at him he gets a strange feeling of recognition of this man.

Ben addresses this person rather nervously,

"Well…welcome to the Riverside Bed and Breakfast Inn, I'll get the manager, plea…please have a seat in our Lobby."

As he often does, Mike comes into the Lobby from the kitchen drying his hands on a dish towel with Ben right behind him. Plain-clothed, U.S. Marshal, Special Agent, Aggelos stands to converse with him,

Mike gets the same feeling of recognition Ben had when he saw him enter, Mike enquires of him,

"Good day Sir, are you looking to stay with us? I have a strange feeling we have met before. Have you ever stayed here with us in the past?"

Mike takes a moment to reflect,

It really feels as if I have met this person before, and that this individual had stayed here for one night in the not-so-distant past but physically looked much different than they do right now, very strange.

"Well, Sir."

Mike interjects,

"Please Sir, just address me as, Mike."

"As yous please, and I am Michael Aggelos."

"So, Mr. Michael Aggelos are you looking for a room with us?"

"Um no, I am here in yourn lovely town heppin' with an investigation of a strange incident that had happened along the River, right near to here a few nights ago."

"Yes our Police Captain John Nichols had come in a few days ago and asked me if I knew anything about it, but there wasn't anything I could tell him that could help his investigation. Sorry. Are you a private investigator here to help the Police?"

"Well Mike, I'm a U.S. Marshal, Special Agent, and yes I'm ah here to hep 'em out with this here case they not to shures to handles."

Mike has a strange recollectioning thought,

Good lord! I do believe, Angel Seraph, was also a U.S. Marshal, Special Agent and she did stay here for one night in the past. Could this be...no, no it can't be, but it feels like it's her to me, but this is a man with the same Southern accent, dear Lord, this is an extremely weird feeling.

"Marshal Aggelos, I have a strong feeling that we have met somehow before."

"Well Mike, I'm ah stayins' at the Ichabod Crain Inn and I does frequent the Horseman Tavern at times, it ah beins' so nearby to me while I'ms ah stayins there. Maybes' we've ah seen each other there?"

Ben with widened eyes gives Mike an inquisitive look.

Mike just shakes his head, in an effort to clear his thoughts and answers him,

"I really don't go there much, this place keeps me rather busy, too busy, much too busy for any real social life. So our meeting there is highly unlikely, and sorry I've nothing that I believe could help you with your investigation."

"Okay then, I's thanks y'all for your time, and yous has yourselves a real nice day now."

And with that said he leaves the Inn.

Ben stands and comes up close to Mike and asks.

"Mike, did you get a...?

"Yup, Ben do I believe, I know what you are going to ask me, and yes I also had a strange feeling about being acquainted with that person before."

Ben, replies,

"I just do hope, the whole day ain't going to be like this."

Ben deeply exhales as he sits back down on the Lobby bench, and Mike also lets out a lengthy exhale, then shrugs his shoulders, looks down at Ben, and smiles at him.

The Lobby door chime sounds off, and instantaneously both Mike and Ben immediately look to see who it is entering, Rachael and Victor enter after they had crossed paths with a strange man going down the deck stairs on his way out of the Lobby when they had together reached the deck floor, they both noticed that the Lobby door was just finishing closing.

Now inside, they both experience a bizarre feeling that something very unusual took place recently within the Inn Lobby.

Victor approaches Mike and inquires,

"Mike everything okay here?"

Mike returns with,

"As well as it can be, Victor, and he continues,

"Well, there was a man just here before you two came in, claiming to be a U.S. Marshal, here to help our local Police with the strange event that happened along the Hudson River Bank a few nights ago, that they were investigating. So our Police, I now believe called into the U.S. Marshals for help with it, because they were a little puzzled and stuck solving it."

Ben, abruptly enters the Lobby holding an open local weekly Newspaper announcing excitedly, it's here, it's here, it's all right here in our Sleepy Hollow Town Cryer Weekly local newspaper!"

"Ben may I see the article please."

"Of course, Victor here you go," he hands the paper to him pointing to the article, "See it's all right there!"

Victor glances at Rachael and quickly reads the piece.

He looks up to all saying,

"It says here, that the Police claim the case has been solved."

Mike questioningly comments,

"Then why was this U.S. Marshal in here asking about it?"

Victor answers him,

"Beats me, Mike!" he quickly glances again at Rachael, "Just might be that there are some unanswered questions, about what happened that night."

"Victor, come on upstairs, walking around the Town with Lucy has made me tired. I could use a little laydown."

"Yup, okay Rach me too, let's go."

Victor hands the paper to Mike and they head up the stairs to their room.

As they walk up the stairs, Rachael softly says to Victor.

"We need to talk about all this."

"Yup, Rach we sure will, but later please, later."

26.

Rachael And Victor enter their room. Rachael suddenly lollops onto the bed letting out a deep sigh. Victor caringly questions her,

"What was that sigh about?"

"Well my love, tomorrow late morning, I will be taking Lucy to the Train Station for her to get back to New York City, and then when I get back, we will need to make a plan to leave here."

Victor questioningly replies to her,

"Leave here! Why?

"Sweetheart, even though the Police report in the local newspaper claims the mysterious case down by the Hudson River has been solved, something surely sounds amiss to me. Like why is this U.S. Marshal still carrying on his investigation?"

"Rachael, I certainly have no idea why he would be."

"It's real simple, my darling, the Police report in the local paper is bogus, just put out so the locals wouldn't panic, and the guilty party may just relax and make a mistake so this U.S. Marshal can most likely catch them in the act of whatever it is that they are doing on the river bank at night."

"You mean us. Right?"

"Of course, I mean us, sweetie, unless there are some others like us here in Sleepy Hollow going around taking people's or animal's Blood until they are lifeless."

Victor laughs at her statement proclaiming,

"I'd think we'd be the first to know that. Right?"

"Of course, we'd be the first and only ones to know if there were any others like us here in this Hamlet of Sleepy Hollow!

"I will go now, to help Lucy to get packed and ready for her return trip and then we three can go down for dinner."

"Okay, I'll get a little rest till you get back here."

"Yup, be back soon, hun."

And with that, she leaves their room.

In Mystic, Connecticut, a car is parked in front of the Cliff House at 30 Cedar Lane. The residents of Cedar Lane while out in the front of their homes, performing some light yard work do take notice of this, but do nothing for the time being. As they continue to watch with acute curiosity, another vehicle comes down the street and parks in the back of the one already there. All of a sudden another vehicle shows up and stops in front of the one that had arrived first.

All of the drivers exit their vehicles at about the same time to gather on the sidewalk in front of the Cedar Lane, Cliff House. The onlooking residents now start to take an extreme interest in these three women, as they start speaking in low tones to each other and keep pointing up at the Cliff House, with introductions then made all around, property owner Mina Di Clerico, realtor Dotty Marshall, and lawyer Linda Madison that represents a group of doctors intending on acquiring the property for diverse medical doctors offices. Dotty gently places her briefcase on the trunk of Mina's car and opens it to get the sales agreement out to be signed.

At this time, one neighborhood resident approached them from one side, while two more approached them from the other side. Mina addresses them all with,

"Hello, may I help all of you?"

One of them speaks up,

"Yes, hello Mrs. DiClerico, we would like to know just what your little gathering is all about, being property-owning residents we have a vested interest in what is happening in our neighborhood mainly to the Cliff House, originally built and owned by the late Mr. Romeo Champa."

Mina explains to them what is happening with the Cliff House, and why they are here. The residents now knowing what will happen to the house, are concerned with any parking for visiting patients. The lawyer steps forward to explain to them that half of the empty lot to the side of the house will be made into a parking lot, which has been cleared by the town to do so.

The residents are pleased to hear this, so they pardon themselves and go back to their respective homes.

Mina looks up at the house one last time, lets out a deep sigh, and then turns to sign all the paperwork, and the three women then return to the vehicles and leave the neighborhood.

In the late morning, after they have had breakfast, Lucy puts her suitcase in the back seat of Rachaels' car in the Inns' parking lot. Gets herself into the passenger seat and buckles up for their ride to the Train Station. Rachael slowly pulls out of the Riverside Inn parking lot onto the road and heads for the station. They chat a little on the way.

"So Lucy did you enjoy yourself up here in Sleepy Hollow?"

"Very much, it truly is an awfully nice area around here!"

"Yup it is," she continues with a lie about them leaving, "but Victor and I will need to leave here soon."

Lucy abruptly inquires,

"Why, Rach?"

Rachael answers her,

"Something to do with Victor's work, I think."

"You think. Don't you know?"

"Not really he doesn't always tell me everything about his work."

"Ooh, a mystery man, very fetch!"

Rachael responds to her calmly,

"Oh yes, a mystery man, for sure."

Lucy giggles at Rachael's response.

"You will contact me when you get to where you are moving to, right?"

"Of course I will, Lucy. We do have each other's e-mail addresses and cell phone numbers."

The train arrives right on time and after a friendly hug on the platform, Lucy steps onto the Train and sits at a window seat where she can see Rachael.

As the Train begins to slowly move down the track, they wave goodbye to one another. Once the Train is out of Rachael's site, she heads out to her car to call Victor. Victor answers her call with,

"Hello hun, Lucy on her way back to New York City?"

"Yes, I'm heading back to you now!"

"Okay, drive safe, see you soon, love you!"

"Love you too, my mystery man!"

"Mystery man?"

"I'll explain when I see you."

27.

Rachael Enters Their room at the Riverside Bed and Breakfast Inn to find Victor at the desk on her laptop, she addresses him cutely and endearingly asking,

"So,... my Mystery Man. What yeah doing?"

"Checking out properties owned by my family's company where we might go to live if we were to leave here. And what's up with this entitling me with, Mystery Man?"

She explains about her talk with Lucy on the ride to the Station about the Mystery Man thing, and Victor just laughs.

"So... my Myst... lover man, what have you found?"

"Actually, there are several places we could go to and live if we wish to, and let me start with my favorite which is Savannah, Georgia, it's the New Orleans of the East Coast, and it is available to us right now, I'd need to put in a request for it sometime today."

"Okay so, what's there for us to reside in, in Savannah, Georgia?"

"Well, there is a fully furnished 12-room Ranch House with two bedrooms and two full bathrooms, near a water tributary that leads right to the ocean, and it looks real nice. Want to have yourself a look-see? You can do a virtual walkthrough," he points to the laptop screen, "right here online."

"Yes, I'll take a look, after we get some lunch."

He agrees and asks,

"Yup, okay, that sounds good to me. Where?"

She inquires

"Where what?"

He answers,

"To have lunch?"

She explains to him, playfully,

"Downstairs in the Inn's dining room, silly!"

"Silly? What happened to Mystery Man?"

She laughs and says,

"I'll freshen up and we can go down for lunch."

"Okay, Babe."

"Babe? What happened to Sweetheart?"

They both laugh as Rachael goes into the bathroom to freshen up.

Down on the first floor of the Inn, Chef Jeannie comes out of the kitchen to the Lobby looking for Benjamin and addresses her brother Mike irately,

"Mike, is Ben in today? If so could you find him I need him in the kitchen pronto."

"Yes, Sis he is here today, I'll see where he is and send him to you asap, so please just chill out!"

She walks away back to the kitchen murmuring,

"That boy is getting more and more…."

Mike walks through the dining area and goes out of the Inn's front door onto the deck, but does not see him so he walks the deck to the side entrance door, and still no Ben, then he notices him walking the parking lot and calls out to him,

"BEN! Benjamen come here right now! Chef Jeannie needs you in the kitchen pronto! What are you doing out here in the parking lot, anyway?"

Ben runs up to the deck stairs, up the three steps, and onto the deck, where he stops in front of Mike and answers the question asked of him,

"I was out here keeping watch for that U.S. Marshal person, just in case he comes back around here asking more questions."

"And just what were you thinking of doing if this Marshal person does show up here again?"

"Running in to give you a heads-up!"

"Oh Ben you're overreacting, Jeannie needs you in the kitchen to help with lunch setups, right this minute, so go in right now, chop chop!"

Ben quickly goes in the side entrance into the Lobby and notices Rachael and Victor at the bottom of the second-floor staircase from where all the rooms of the Inn are.

He addresses them, figuring they are coming down to have some lunch,

"Hello, my two favorite guests, if you're looking for lunch I think it's gonna' be a little bit late, so sorry it's my fault. Please be patient."

Rachael empathetically answers him,

"No prob my boy, we'll just go for a little walk, after all, it is a beautiful slightly overcast day!"

Victor chimes in,

"No sweat kid, we'll be back later, so to give you some more time."

Ben walks away from them to the kitchen, with a thought of,

A beautiful slightly overcast day, some adults are very strange in what they consider a nice day to be outside.

As Rachael and Victor leisurely stroll along the sidewalks of Sleepy Hollow, Rachael speaks softly asking Victor,

"So how do you figure we do the move?"

"Okay, then I guess we are actually going to leave here."

"The way I see it, Victor, we don't have much of a choice. Now do we?"

"I guess you are right, after all, you know more about dealing with the way we need to live and survive, than I do."

"Yup, unfortunately, I do, but it's also fortunate that I do. So how do you suggest we perform our re-location?"

Okay, I do want to keep my Harley, so we can hire a Pod-like thing to transport it and the stuff we need to take along with us, and you and I can just drive down in your car."

"Good, sounds like a perfect plan, I can take care of anything else that needs to be done. And after lunch, I'll have a look at the house which I most likely think I'll like, so you then can secure it for us to live there."

"Once I've secured it for us, we can leave here and move in when we'd like to."

"And when the time comes, I'll deal with Mike about us leaving and the money situation for our having stayed here.

Okay, now Victor, so let's get back to the Inn now, and have our lunch first."

"Good because I'm feeling rather peckish right now, for one of Chef Jeannies delicious, what she calls a lunch waffle! Sure, am going to, miss her cooking!"

"Oh yes, me too!"

28.

Rachael And Victor get back to the Inn, just in time to be seated for luncheon. After having another one of Jeannies' delicious luncheon meals, they retire to their room, so that Rachael can do a virtual walkthrough, on her laptop, of the Ranch House in Savannah. She likes the floor plan very much but would like to change some of the furnishings and also some of the decor. Victor agrees with her that some of the things are out of date and do need to be changed. She becomes very excited and stands up to proclaim,

"Please Victor, let's go live there as soon as we can, we should start the moving procedure as early as tomorrow, please!"

"Rachael, let me first secure the house for us on my family's company's property website right now, by using my name and Social Security number, so we will get to move in as soon as we can get there. But first, the prepping of it will start."

Curiously Rachael inquires,

"The prepping of it?"

"Yes, sweetheart the general manager for this house will need to be contacted and told to send in a crew to do an inspection of the house and estate, to make sure all the utilities are working properly and up to the most recent state codes, and that the terrain has been properly manicured. Also, the company's legal department will draw up the paperwork to be signed by my father and me for us to be the permanent occupants. It should take a few days or so. I will need to give them your E-Mail address for it to happen online which will make it go faster. So just relax, please."

"Okay, Victor just get it going, like yesterday!"

At her somewhat silly remark, Victor laughs a little and, replies

"Rachael, that's not being relaxed."

"I know, I am a little contrite, my love, I just want us to get out of Sleepy Hollow, as soon as we are able to do so, is all! I don't feel safe here anymore, just like when I was in the Cliff House in Mystic Connecticut, and desired to leave there too."

"We will, Rachael, we will, so please chill out and let me get the ball rolling on this. Okay?"

"Yes, Victor my love, I'm awfully sorry for being so impatient! I didn't know or realize what it would take for you to do this."

"It's okay, I understand where you are coming from. And I do sympathize with the way you are feeling."

He takes her in his arms to comfort her, with a sincere attempt to make her feel safe and secure. His doing this causes her to let out a deep sigh of relief. When he releases her from his comforting hug she walks over to the bed and lollops on to it. He sits back down at the laptop and sends her E-Mail to the proper person who will need it, to send him the paperwork needing to be signed by him and also sent to his father, for his signature.

Victor moves to the bed and sits on the edge, Rachael feels the bed move and turns over to him, right away he takes note that she is looking a little pale so he inquires,

"Rach, are you feeling okay you do look a little pale to me?"

"I know, I could use a Blood feeding from a large animal. How are you doing, Victor?"

Me? I'm feeling okay for now but just might need one also before we head down to Georgia. So I'll have Ben bring you something to our room for you to eat for your dinner maybe there'll be some of Jeannie's Tomato Soup you like so much, and then later when it starts to get dark, we can both go to the small clearing I had found downriver, where I did happen to notice some large animal tracks along the river bank. I will accompany you to keep watch, while you get your feeding."

"That sounds doable my love, I'll just rest awhile, so you can go down to have your dinner and tell Ben to bring me something to my room to have for my dinner."

"Hopefully some of that Tomato Soup you love so much."

She turns over away from him making the Yum sound.

He rises slowly from the bed and walks to the bathroom to freshen up to go down for his dinner, thinking,

This is no way for anyone to live, even people like us, what we need, is perhaps a miracle of some sort. Maybe, just maybe…

And with that, his thinking trails off.

He leans in to softly kiss Rachael on her cheek and then quietly leaves the room. In the dining room, Victor is seated, by the hostess Kathy at a small table for two, Ben arrives with a water pitcher and caringly asks,

"Just you tonight Victor, or is Rachael coming down soon?"

Victor looks up at him and explains,

"Well, Ben my boy, she is in our room, not feeling well. If you would please bring her a bowl of Chef Jeannie's wonderful Tomato Soup, if there is any, I mean."

"Well, Victor it's not on the menu tonight, but I do believe there is a small amount leftover from last night just enough for one serving, which I could warm up and bring up to her asap!"

"That would be just great, Ben just be sure to go in quietly and put it on the desk."

"Yup, and I'll put it in a special bowl that will keep it warm for her, and we do have some nice fresh French bread, to go with it."

"That would be so nice of you Ben, you are a real treasure!"

"Thank you, Sir... I mean Victor. Your waitress will be with you shortly, and by the way, there is a fab Pot Roast dinner tonight, I happened to have sneaked a taste for myself of it earlier and it's really awesome!"

29.

Victor Returns To their room to find, on the desk an empty soup bowl, spoon, and a small plate with some bread crumbs in it, also an empty wine glass, then looks over to the bed to find that Rachael is not in it, he then hears the shower in the bathroom turn on and realizes that it's Rachael getting cleaned up for her Blood-feeding trip to the Hudson Riverbank, later. He sits at the desk after moving the bowl with the spoon in it, dish, and wine glass out of the way and opens the laptop to find that it's on a furniture and decor web page. He then hears the shower shut off and then a minute or so later, he hears a blow dryer turn on. He checks the E-Mail account to see if their occupancy document for him to sign, has come in. It has not arrived, as of yet, so he thinks,

Most likely it will come in tomorrow,

and jokily adds in his thoughts,

Not yesterday!

He disconnects from the E-Mail page and then closes the Laptop, just as Rachael comes out of the bathroom, she notices him and articulates,

"Victor your back. How was your dinner?"

"It was quite awesome, you missed a good one, Chef Jeannie's delicious Pot Roast dinner! Did you enjoy the soup, I had Ben take up to you?"

"Yes, I was very much grateful to you and Ben for doing that for me, as you know, I was in no condition to go down for dinner tonight!"

"No prob Sweetheart, now just let me know when you want to go down to the Riverbank."

"Okay, but I'd like to wait until the dinner hour is over and things do settle down a bit on the first floor of the Inn."

"It is almost over, and besides we can go out the side door opposite the one that leads to the parking lot."

"My thinking exactly, great minds do think alike, my love!"

"Yup, but I think you mean devious minds. Right?"

"Yes, Victor, per say, my dear, I was just trying to sound more civil than evil."

"People like us don't have much of that in our lives if we want to survive, that is."

"Correct Victor, but oftentimes the Human side of, as you say, people like us, will come out for us."

"Yes, my sweet, I do agree with that, but it will only come out after our inhumane survival deed has been performed, which is much too late to change, what we had to do to a human or an animal for our existence for the kind of people we… you and I are."

"Victor my love, we surely could use a miracle in our lives!"

"My thoughts exactly, my dear!"

With a large beautiful full moon low in the sky, Rachael and Victor leave the Inn the way they had agreed to so no one would see them going out, and quickly reach Riverside Road and cross over, where they begin walking parallel to the Hudson River away from the Inn, in the direction of the wooded Hudson Riverbank smaller clearing, that Victor found and has used only once for a Blood Passion feeding. Victor suddenly stops walking, and by pointing, directs Rachael to go into the woods to the small clearing. Not being too familiar with this part of the Riverbank, she removes from her pocket a small pen flashlight to guide her footing, she carefully proceeds into the wooded Riverbank, while Victor stays out on the grassy embankment along the road to keep watch. He nervously paces, and suddenly hears and sees a two-wheel, one-headlight vehicle, and recognizes the sound of a Harley Davidson motorcycle, coming down the road in his direction.

This rider pulls over onto the grassy embankment just a few yards before Victor, dismounts the bike, and begins to walk toward him. Victor thinks,

A lost traveler wanting directions perhaps?

As this rider approaches closer, they remove their helmet to reveal in the bright Moonlight to be a man, he also realizes that Victor is also male and says,

"Good evenin' Sir, rather a pretty night for ah walkin'."

"Good evening, it certainly is especially after a grand meal."

"Might you Sir, be lost and looking for help?"

"Not at all Sir, just on my patrol!"

"On patrol? Are you a local law Officer out of uniform?"

"Not local law, no, I'ms' a U.S. Marshal in this area hepin' the local Police with a rather suspicious case, is all."

Victor is suddenly struck with a strange thought, along with a rather weird feeling,

That southern accent, a U.S. Marshal and not from around here, I'm getting a really strange feeling of recognition, but there is no way it could be who I am feeling it could be, strange very much stranger, after all this is a man and she was a... this is crazy, barmy, really weird, might just be my nerves.

The Marshal interrupts Victor's thinking with,

"Well, Sir, ain't it just amazin' how the full moon reflects off the water makins' it ta look like, a beam of light is comins' threw them there trees along that there beautiful Hudson River you have up here's in these parts?"

"Yes, it most certainly does, and kind of pretty too, Marshal, almost like someone is in there with a flashlight, pointing it out onto the road."

Looking harder now into the wooded area the Marshal concurs,

"I kinda agrees' with ya'll, but I don't sees me anyone in there. By the way," extending his hand to Victor he continues,

"Howdy to y'all, Sir, mys' official title and full name is U.S. Marshal Michael Aggelos. And you Sir are?"

Victor hesitates before answering him,

"Oh me..., yes, I'm Victor, very nice to have met you, Marshal Aggelos."

They then shake hands,

"Well, Victor I'll's be on my way now, it's beins' real nice haveins' meetins' y'all, you has yourselfs' a real nice after dinna' walkins'."

"Thanks, Marshal Aggelos, I will, and the feeling is mutual."

And he adds in his mind,

And rather strange.

As the U.S. Marshal walks back to his Harley he ponders,

That light from the full moon reflecting on the river water, and coming threw the trees like it did tonight, most likely was what that motorist saw and reported, from the road that evening in question. I guess this case for me is now finally closed.

Reaching his Bike he turns it around and heads back up the road the way he came. He will notify the local Police Captain that he is done with this case here and then contact the U.S. Marshals' Department main office to inform them that he is finished up here in Sleepy Hollow and then get the arrangements for him to get back to the U.S. Marshal's Department offices there in the Supreme Court building in Washington DC to file his official report.

Victor now continues his pacing and breathes a sigh of relief. In his mind he confirms,

I don't believe that telling Racheal that the U.S. Marshal came by and I had contact with him, would be a good idea, she's on edge enough already, so not mentioning it happening would be the best thing for our situation, right now.

He is brought out of his thoughts by Rachael appearing from the trees and onto the embankment. He acknowledges her,

"Rachael, how'd it go, you okay?"

With the moonlight now illuminating her face, he lovingly comments,

"You do look much better."

"It went just the way I've done it before and yes I do feel much better now!"

"Well let's get back to our room, I want to see if that residence E-Mail for me to sign came in yet. Then we could order the Pod and make our arrangements to be on our way to Savanah, Georgia, real soon."

"Oh, Victor I'd very much love that, I would!"

He extends his hand to her and says,

"I know, so come on let us get going back to our room!"

She takes his hand and collectively they jovially make their way back to the Riverside Inn and then up to their room.

Now up in their room, Rachael sits on the edge of the bed and proclaims,

"It's still somewhat of a rush to have a Blood feeding although only from an animal, and not from a human!"

Now in her sleeping attire, she lollops backward onto the bed and closes her eyes letting out a deep sigh and shifting herself to be in the sleeping posture, rolls herself over to her side of the bed, and then falls off to sleep.

Victor, now at the desk, opens the Laptop to find the E-mail he has been expecting has finally come in. He electronically signs his name to it and sends it back, then closes the Laptop and excitedly turns in his chair to inform Rachael, but she has fallen off to sleep and will not hear him, so he just thinks,

I really should let her sleep, and then tell her in the morning when she wakes up.

So for now, he'll be patient and let her sleep through the rest of the night. And get for himself some sleep as well.

30.

In The Mid-morning, Victor wakes, uses the bathroom, and then comes out to happily find Rachael awake and sitting up in bed, slowly he approaches her, then walks around to her side of the bed, and sits on the edge, looking at her, taking her hand and smiling a big smile. Looking at him she asks and proclaims,

"Why you smiling like that? It's rather creepy!"

"I have some wonderous news you are simply going to love!"

"Yeah, and what wonderful news is that, my dearest?"

"Okay, so I signed the occupancy document last night while you were asleep, so now we can move into the house in Savanah, Georgia whenever we'd like to!"

She smiles at him and then throws her arms around him happily saying,

"Oh my, Victor that's so absolutely wonderful!"

And she kisses him with deep joyful emotion.

He continues with,

"And I have made contact with the local mobile Pods Moving Company and they can have one here in a day or two for us. We just need to give them a one-day notice and tell them what size we will need."

"Victor, that means I will need to speak with Mike rather soon about us leaving the Riverside Bed and Breakfast Inn. If there is any money overlapping in the pre-paid residing account I will handle that agreement between Mike and me, on what to do about it."

"Of course, you will, after all our living here is in yours' and your cousins' names, so that's on you, to handle any way you see fit to, my dear."

"Victor you have made me so very happy, if it's at all possible I love you even more for you doing this for us!"

"As far, Rachael, as I could and now can tell we have no choice, although…"

He hesitates and thinks,

Like I thought last night, there really is no need or reason to tell her about that U.S. Marshal showing up on Riverside Road when she was in the clearing getting a Blood feeding from an animal.

"Victor, although what?"

"Never mind my dear, nothing very pertinent to our leaving, and yes I do wholeheartedly agree with you that we very much do need to relocate ourselves, things seem to be getting a little hot around here, so we need to go asap. Right?"

"Yes, Victor, my love, I say the day after tomorrow, we should be good to go, so we will need to call the Pod Company to deliver one here soon."

"Rachael, my although is, I do feel sad about leaving all these nice people and this lovely town of Sleepy Hollow, up here in this big State of New York."

"Rachael, you think this state is big, just wait till you see and live in Georgia!"

"Victor, how much bigger is the state of Georgia than the state of New York?"

"I'd have to say about two to two and a half times larger!"

"Wow, really?"

"Yes, my dear now we should get us some breakfast, so why don't you get up and dressed so we can go down for something to eat, for our morning meal here at least one of our last times."

"Yes, I will."

Rachael gets out of bed, and on her way to the bathroom she continues with,

"I am, feeling a little bit hungry this morning."

As she passes by Victor on her way to get ready, he gives her a loving soft pat on her bum.

She exclaims,

"Oooh, Vic!"

He answers,

"Feeling very much hungry this morning, myself!"

Seated now for their breakfast they order, and speak softly to each other,

"Victor after we eat I will start to pack up for us both."

"Sounds like a great start. While you do that I'll call for the pod to be delivered tomorrow afternoon, there should be room in the Inn parking lot for it and the following morning we can head south."

"Victor, I am so happy, I have not been his happy in a long time!"

He leans over close to her and softly informs her,

"Tonight, I'll get myself a Blood feeding like you did last night, it should sustain me for our trip."

"Do you need me to go with you, to keep watch?"

"No, Rach I'll be fine."

"Okay if you say so."

"I do, sweetheart."

With that said their food is served, so they go about enjoying breakfast together.

After their morning meal, they return to their room to begin packing for the trip south. Victor on the laptop orders a Pod to be delivered to the Riverside Bed and Breakfast Inn Parking lot on the Riverside Road in Sleepy Hollow, of the size he tells them they will need, for tomorrow afternoon. Rachael goes down to speak with Mike about their leaving the day after tomorrow. After about twenty minutes she returns, Victor asks her how it went, and she informs him,

"Well, Mike was sad to have us suddenly leaving, and about the room rental we still had a two-months-ahead payment on it."

"So did you ask him for a refund?"

"No, Vic, I didn't, I told him because he, his sister, Chef Jeannie, Ben, and all the rest of the Inn staff, were so wonderful and so accommodating to my cousin Mia and us, to keep it as a generous tip and also use some of it to give to Ben only to help to further his education."

"Wow! That is very, very generous of you to do that!"

"I know and it made me feel wonderful to be able to do it for them because between, my money and yours, we have more than enough for the move and to live on, and if we need more we could start some kind of business for ourselves in Savanah."

"Yes, we could and I already have an idea about doing that, actually the A.B. Ladies Shop gave me the idea of doing something similar like it someday."

"Sounds to me like a great idea and I'd be more than happy to help with the running of it in any way I could."

"Yup, sometimes it would take the two of us to run it."

"Mmm, a nice family business."

"Tonight I'll go to the clearing, for you know what! And we can load up the Pod tomorrow afternoon and can be on our way in the morning the next day."

"Victor, I'm sure Ben will be of help to us."

"Although, Rach he may be rather broken-hearted that we are leaving."

"Yup I believe he will, but I'll tell him we will keep in touch by E-Mail and cellphone calls. That should make him feel better."

"Yes, I think that he will find solace in the idea of you and him doing that with each other from time to time."

On the morning of their last full day in Sleepy Hollow they have breakfast in the dining room of the Riverside Bed and Breakfast Inn, Chef Jeannie now knowing they will be leaving soon, presents them with a morning meal fit for a King and a Queen. They are more than thrilled, and very appreciative, but also a little sad. The moving mobile Pod should be delivered later today in the early afternoon. Ben comes meekly to their table with a fresh piping hot pot of coffee to top their cups off. He announces,

"Victor and Rachael, it has been my great pleasure to be of service to you both and Rachael also to your author cousin Mia, when she was with us here at the Inn, I have missed her, and I will miss you both just as much, maybe even more. Now if you two would allow me, I will be happy to be of assistance in helping get your things out to the parking lot and into that Pod thing."

Chef Jeannie comes out of the kitchen and over to their table to tell them,

"For your leaving, on your trip early tomorrow morning I will pre-pack you both a basket of foods that I know you each love."

They both thank her, and she heads back to her kitchen, giving them a teary goodbye.

Now finished with the meal they head up to their room to do the final packing of what will be needed to be put into the Pod. Their most personal items and some of their clothes in suitcases will be riding with them in Rachaels' car.

Very early the following morning with the Pod holding Victor's refurbished classic Harley-Davidson Motorcycle securely and some of their other things, in the parking lot Rachael puts in her car the last of their things to go with them along with the food basket from Jeannie. Hugs and cheek kisses along with handshakes are had all around, with Victor in the driver's seat before entering her car Rachael stands at the open passenger door and takes one last look at the place that has been her home for quite a while, for both her altered identification of Mia Harkness and for her real self, Rachael Valli, and with a tear on her cheek she enters the car and they drive off out of the lot and head down the road south. About thirty minutes later a vehicle comes to pick up the Pod that will be delivered to their new fully furnished home at their address in Savanah, Georgia.

After driving for several hours they decide, at about one pm to make a rest stop for a bathroom break and to have some of the food in the basket Jeannie had given to them for the trip, so Victor pulls off the highway into a rest area that has restrooms and what looks like a small picnic area. After about thirty minutes of rest, they get back on the road with Rachael driving now, not too far up ahead they notice a vehicle hauling a Pod on it, thinking it just might be theirs. The G.P.S. tells them they have about another six-hour drive to their destination. They should arrive there at about eight pm. The cases in the car have their sleeping attire and a change of clothes, emptying the Pod would be done the following day and then call to have the Pod picked up.

They arrived at about eight thirty at the house, with the Pod in the driveway, Rachael parks on the street in front of the house. Sluggishly they take the suitcases out of the car and make their way up the walkway and after finding the door key under the nome beside the door they enter the house. They both lollop on the couch letting out a deep sigh.

"Rach, what do you say we go to bed and tackle the Pod in the morning?"

"Hunny, I'm with you, yes!"

"Okay, good cause I'm beat."

They both quickly fall off into a deep sleep, unnoticed and unseen by them a large oval of golden light appears outside above the house, inside the oval is a very faint image of a man's face, and then from the golden light a tapered beam of gold shines down through the roof, and into their bedroom, it moves slowly over to sleeping Rachaels' chest, it hovers there for while, she stirs a little but does not wake, slowly and painlessly a black mist is drawn out from her chest, then the beam moves over to Victor's chest and the same thing takes place. The two black misty clouds diminish within the golden beam of light and are gone. A silent stillness ruminates in their room and throughout the whole house. All is peaceful and tranquil.

Unknown to them, a magnificent miracle has been granted and taken place while they slept soundly, and now they are both reborn as normal humans, the Vampireisem has departed from their bodies this very night, and forever after.

The sun shines through the window onto Rachael's face and she feels no pain from it, she rolls over to Victor and touching him says,

"Vic, wake up something has happened but I'm not sure just what, wake up, please. Vic wake up!"

He stirs and turns his face to hers answering her with,

"Yup, my darlins' I'ms awake now, what is it gots you all riled up?"

"Victor don't you hear yourself, your…your Georgian southern accent has returned!"

"Well, what do ya knows, it is, dang it is!'

"And try as I might, I can't bring out any of the Vampire attributes I had! Isn't it wonderful we can now live as regular people being married and having children!"

Rachael jumps up out of bed.

"Victor, Victor get up it's, it's a miracle a wonderful and fantastic miracle!"

She stops celebrating, takes a breath, and has a quick thankful thought,

Thank you, dear father, my beloved late father, Michael Valli, I love you even more for this.

Epilogue

Victor And Rachael have been enjoying their married lives together in Savanah, Georgia for several years now, just as normal persons would do, and being parents, blessed with having healthy fraternal twins; a boy, Michael, and a girl, Carmella.

Victor had, as he had said he would, opened a men's clothing shop in the downtown area, with his family's long-time textile business he already has unlimited contacts for buying stock for the store, which he entitled, by using his family name, Vincent's Men Shop, which has been doing rather well for some time now. While Rachael has been performing the somewhat and sometimes challenging life of an adoring wife to Victor and a loving mother to their children. They are very happy living as a blissful normal family and do feel very blessed to be doing so.

Their atrocious past lives as Hybrid Vampires seems to them to be like a million years ago, very much forgotten, dead, and buried in their past, to be never ever spoken of to each other or anyone. The only thing they want and pray for is to be happy in a long and fulfilled life together, until death by natural causes separates them from each other.

Oh and yes, Rachael's long-time girlfriend Lucy Howard, now Mrs. Lucy Nelson, is the Godmother to their children, along with Victor's younger brother Vernon Vincent, who is their Godfather.

Lucy has visited with them many times, accompanied by her husband, John Nelson, and their two children, having moved to and living close by in the city of Louisville, Georgia.

So, as it has been pronounced in so many story endings:
'And they all lived happily ever after!'

Fini.

J.M. VALENTE's Published Novels

'BLOOD PASSION'
~Novels Series~

VOLUME ONE
Containing:
Books: I, II, III, and the Prequel
Book IV, and Book V

Also Available:
Autobiography - *The Time of My Lives*

~~~~~~~~

All Available at:
amazon.com

Available in **Paperback**, **Hardcover**, and **E-Book** formats

Contact E-Mail:
jimvalente@comcast.net

www.ingramcontent.com/pod-product-compliance
Lightning Source LLC
LaVergne TN
LVHW021959060526
838201LV00048B/1631